THE QUEEN'S CLASSICS

LOVE OF LIFE
And other stories by Jack London

THE QUEEN'S CLASSICS

General Editor: DENYS THOMPSON, M.A.

LOVE OF LIFE

and other stories by

JACK LONDON

Selected by
Denys Thompson

Chatto and Windus

LONDON

Published by
Chatto & Windus (Educational) Ltd
42 William IV Street
London WC2

*

Clarke, Irwin and Co Ltd
Toronto

SBN 7010 0384 7

First published in Queen's Classics 1968
Selection and Introduction
Copyright © Denys Thompson 1968
Printed in Great Britain by
Cox and Wyman Ltd
London, Fakenham and Reading

CONTENTS

The Author

John Griffith London was born at San Francisco in 1876. He had a most wretched childhood, and from the age of eleven earned his own living by odd jobs; at fifteen he was working ten hours a day or more in a canning factory. He took to oyster poaching, and bought his own sloop while still in his teens. He soon changed sides, and joined the Fish Patrol that protected the oyster beds. After a spell of seal-hunting he joined 'Kelly's Army'—a march of the unemployed upon Washington in 1894—and became a socialist. He took part in the gold rush to the Klondike in 1898–99, but found no gold.

However what he did find was that he could make money by writing stories. He was engaged as a war correspondent to report the South African War, and went to London en route for Africa. He never reached it, because the job collapsed under him, so he took the opportunity to study the slums of London. He found them as bad as an earlier investigator, Henry Mayhew, had revealed them to be, and wrote up his findings in *People of the Abyss*. His best-known works followed— *Call of the Wild* in 1903, and *White Fang* in 1906. He ruined a splendid constitution by drink and drugs, and died in 1916.

Love of Life

This out of all will remain—
They have lived and have tossed:
So much of the game will be gain,
Though the gold of the dice has been lost.

THEY limped painfully down the bank, and once the foremost of the two men staggered among the rough-strewn rocks. They were tired and weak, and their faces had the drawn expression of patience which comes of hardship long endured. They were heavily burdened with blanket packs which were strapped to their shoulders. Head straps, passing across the forehead, helped support these packs. Each man carried a rifle. They walked in a stooped posture, the shoulders well forward, the head still farther forward, the eyes bent upon the ground.

'I wish we had just about two of them cartridges that's layin' in that cache of ourn,' said the second man.

His voice was utterly and drearily expressionless. He spoke without enthusiasm; and the first man, limping into the milky stream that foamed over the rocks, vouchsafed no reply.

The other man followed at his heels. They did not remove their footgear, though the water was icy cold—so cold that their ankles ached and their feet went numb. In places the water dashed against their knees, and both men staggered for footing.

The man who followed slipped on a smooth boulder, nearly fell, but recovered himself with a violent effort, at the same time uttering a sharp exclamation of pain. He seemed faint and dizzy and put out his free hand while he reeled, as though seeking support against the air. When he had steadied himself he stepped forward, but reeled again and nearly fell. Then he stood still and looked at the other man, who had never turned his head.

The man stood still for fully a minute, as though debating with himself. Then he called out:

'I say, Bill, I've sprained my ankle.'

Bill staggered on through the milky water. He did not look around. The man watched him go, and though his face was expressionless as ever, his eyes were like the eyes of a wounded deer.

The other man limped up the farther bank and continued straight on without looking back. The man in the stream watched him. His lips trembled a little, so that the rough thatch of brown hair which covered them was visibly agitated. His tongue even strayed out to moisten them.

'Bill!' he cried out.

It was the pleading cry of a strong man in distress, but Bill's head did not turn. The man watched him go, limping grotesquely and lurching forward with stammering gait up the slow slope towards the soft sky-line of the low-lying hill. He watched him go till he passed over the crest and disappeared. Then he turned his gaze and slowly took in the circle of the world that remained to him now that Bill was gone.

Near the horizon the sun was smouldering dimly, almost obscured by formless mists and vapours, which gave an impression of mass and density without outline or tangibility. The man pulled out his watch, the while resting his weight on one leg. It was four o'clock, and as the season was near the last of July or first of August—he did not know the precise date within a week or two—he knew that the sun roughly marked the north-west. He looked to the south and knew that somewhere beyond those bleak hills lay the Great Bear Lake; also, he knew that in that direction the Arctic Circle cut its forbidding way across the Canadian Barrens. This stream in which he stood was a feeder to the Coppermine River, which in turn flowed north and emptied into Coronation Gulf and the Arctic Ocean. He had never been there, but he had seen it, once, on a Hudson's Bay Company chart.

Again his gaze completed the circle of the world about him. It was not a heartening spectacle. Everywhere was soft skyline.

The hills were all low-lying. There were no trees, no shrubs, no grasses—naught but a tremendous and terrible desolation that sent fear swiftly dawning into his eyes.

'Bill!' he whispered, once and twice; 'Bill!'

He cowered in the midst of the milky water, as though the vastness were pressing in upon him with overwhelming force, brutally crushing him with its complacent awfulness. He began to shake as with an ague fit, till the gun fell from his hand with a splash. This served to rouse him. He fought with his fear and pulled himself together, groping in the water and recovering the weapon. He hitched his pack farther over on his left shoulder, so as to take a portion of its weight from off the injured ankle. Then he proceeded, slowly and carefully, wincing with pain, to the bank.

He did not stop. With a desperation that was madness, unmindful of the pain, he hurried up the slope to the crest of the hill over which his comrade had disappeared—more grotesque and comical by far than that limping, jerking comrade. But at the crest he saw a shallow valley, empty of life. He fought with his fear again, overcame it, hitched the pack still farther over on his left shoulder, and lurched on down the slope.

The bottom of the valley was soggy with water, which the thick moss held, spongelike, close to the surface. This water squirted out from under his feet at every step, and each time he lifted a foot the action culminated in a sucking sound as the wet moss reluctantly released its grip. He picked his way from muskeg to muskeg, and followed the other man's footsteps along and across the rocky ledges which thrust like islets through the sea of moss.

Though alone, he was not lost. Farther on, he knew, he would come to where dead spruce and fir, very small and wizened, bordered the shore of a little lake, the *titchinnichilie*, in the tongue of the country, the 'land of little sticks'. And into that lake flowed a small stream, the water of which was not milky. There was rush grass on that stream—this he remembered well— but no timber, and he would follow it till its first trickle ceased at a divide. He would cross this divide to the first trickle of another stream, flowing to the west, which he would follow until it emptied into the river Dease, and here he would find a cache under an upturned canoe and piled over with many rocks. And in this cache would be ammunition for his empty gun, fish-hooks and lines, a small net—all the utilities for the killing and snaring of food. Also he would find flour—not much—a piece of bacon, and some beans.

Bill would be waiting for him there, and they would paddle away south down the Dease to the Great Bear Lake. And south across the lake they would go, ever south, till they gained the Mackenzie. And south, still south, they would go, while the winter raced vainly after them, and the ice formed in the eddies, and the days grew chill and crisp, south to some warm Hudson's Bay Company post, where timber grew tall and generous and there was grub without end.

These were the thoughts of the man as he strove onward. But hard as he strove with his body, he strove equally hard with his mind, trying to think that Bill had not deserted him, that Bill would surely wait for him at the cache. He was compelled to think this thought, or else there would not be any use to strive, and he would have lain down and died. And as the dim ball of the sun sank slowly into the north-west he covered every inch—and many times—of his and Bill's flight south before the down-coming winter. And he conned the grub of the cache and the grub of the Hudson's Bay Company post over and over again. He had not eaten for two days; for a far longer time he had not had all he wanted to eat. Often he stooped and picked pale muskeg berries, put them into his mouth, and chewed and swallowed them. A muskeg berry is a bit of seed enclosed in a bit of water. In the mouth the water melts away and the seed chews sharp and bitter. The man knew there was no nourishment in the berries, but he chewed them patiently with a hope greater than knowledge and defying experience.

At nine o'clock he stubbed his toe on a rocky ledge, and from sheer weariness and weakness staggered and fell. He lay for some time, without movement, on his side. Then he slipped out of his pack straps and clumsily dragged himself into a sitting posture. It was not yet dark, and in the lingering twilight he groped about among the rocks for shreds of dry moss. When he had gathered a heap he built a fire—a smouldering, smudgy fire—and put a tin pot of water on to boil.

He unwrapped his pack and the first thing he did was to count his matches. There were sixty-seven. He counted them three times to make sure. He divided them into several portions, wrapping them in oil paper, disposing of one bunch in his empty tobacco pouch, of another bunch in the inside band of his battered hat, of a third bunch under his shirt on the chest. This accomplished, a panic came upon him, and he unwrapped them all and counted them again. There were still sixty-seven.

He dried his wet footgear by the fire. The moccasins were in soggy shreds. The blanket socks were worn through in places, and his feet were raw and bleeding. His ankle was throbbing, and he gave it an examination. It had swollen to the size of his knee. He tore a long strip from one of his two blankets and bound the ankle tightly. He tore other strips and bound them about his feet to serve for both moccasins and socks. Then he drank the pot of water, steaming hot, wound his watch, and crawled between his blankets.

He slept like a dead man. The brief darkness around midnight came and went. The sun arose in the north-east—at least the day dawned in that quarter, for the sun was hidden by grey clouds.

At six o'clock he awoke, quietly lying on his back. He gazed straight up into the grey sky and knew that he was hungry. As he rolled over on his elbow he was startled by a loud snort, and saw a bull caribou regarding him with alert curiosity. The animal was not more than fifty feet away, and instantly into the man's mind leaped the vision and the savour of a caribou steak sizzling and frying over a fire. Mechanically he reached for the empty gun, drew a bead, and pulled the trigger. The bull snorted and leaped away, his hoofs rattling and clattering as he fled across the ledges.

The man cursed and flung the empty gun from him. He groaned aloud as he started to drag himself to his feet. It was a slow and arduous task. His joints were like rusty hinges. They worked harshly in their sockets, with much friction, and each bending and unbending was accomplished only through a sheer exertion of will. When he finally gained his feet, another minute or so was consumed in straightening up, so that he could stand erect as a man should stand.

He crawled up a small knoll and surveyed the prospect. There were no trees, no bushes, nothing but a grey sea of moss scarcely diversified by grey rocks, grey lakelets, and grey streamlets. The sky was grey. There was no sun nor hint of sun. He had no idea of north, and he had forgotten the way he had come to this spot the night before. But he was not lost. He knew that. Soon he would come to the land of the little sticks. He felt that it lay off to the left somewhere, not far— possibly just over the next low hill.

He went back to put his pack into shape for travelling. He assured himself of the existence of his three separate parcels of matches, though he did not stop to count them. But he did linger, debating, over a squat moose-hide sack. It was not large. He could hide it under his two hands. He knew that it weighed fifteen pounds—as much as all the rest of the pack— and it worried him. He finally set it to one side and proceeded to roll the pack. He paused to gaze at the squat moose-hide sack. He picked it up hastily with a defiant glance about him, as though the desolation were trying to rob him of it; and when he rose to his feet to stagger on into the day, it was included in the pack on his back.

He bore away to the left, stopping now and again to eat muskeg berries. His ankle had stiffened, his limp was more pronounced, but the pain of it was as nothing compared with the pain of his stomach. The hunger pangs were sharp. They gnawed and gnawed until he could not keep his mind steady on the course he must pursue to gain the land of little sticks.

The muskeg berries did not allay this gnawing, while they made his tongue and the roof of his mouth sore with their irritating bite.

He came upon a valley where rock ptarmigan rose on whirring wings from the ledges and muskegs. 'Ker—ker—ker' was the cry they made. He threw stones at them, but could not hit them. He placed his pack on the ground and stalked them as a cat stalks a sparrow. The sharp rocks cut through his pants' legs till his knees left a trail of blood; but the hurt was lost in the hurt of his hunger. He squirmed over the wet moss, saturating his clothes and chilling his body; but he was not aware of it, so great was his fever for food. And always the ptarmigan rose, whirring, before him, till their 'ker—ker—ker' became a mock to him, and he cursed them and cried aloud at them with their own cry.

Once he crawled upon one that must have been asleep. He did not see it till it shot up in his face from its rocky nook. He made a clutch as startled as was the rise of the ptarmigan, and there remained in his hand three tail feathers. As he watched its flight he hated it, as though it had done him some terrible wrong. Then he returned and shouldered his pack.

As the day wore along he came into valleys or swales where game was more plentiful. A band of caribou passed by, twenty and odd animals, tantalizingly within rifle range. He felt a wild desire to run after them, a certitude that he could run them down. A black fox came towards him, carrying a ptarmigan in his mouth. The man shouted. It was a fearful cry, but the fox, leaping away in fright, did not drop the ptarmigan.

Late in the afternoon he followed a stream, milky with lime, which ran through sparse patches of rush grass. Grasping these rushes firmly near the root, he pulled up what resembled a young onion sprout no larger than a shingle nail. It was tender, and his teeth sank into it with a crunch that promised deliciously of food. But its fibres were tough. It was composed of stringy filaments saturated with water, like the berries, and devoid of nourishment. He threw off his pack and went into the rush grass on hands and knees, crunching and munching, like some bovine creature.

He was very weary and often wished to rest—to lie down and sleep; but he was continually driven on—not so much by his desire to gain the land of little sticks as by his hunger. He searched little ponds for frogs and dug up the earth with his nails for worms, though he knew in spite that neither frogs nor worms existed so far north.

He looked into every pool of water vainly, until, as the long twilight came on, he discovered a solitary fish, the size of a minnow, in such a pool. He plunged his arm in up to the shoulder, but it eluded him. He reached for it with both hands and stirred up the milky mud at the bottom. In his excitement he fell in, wetting himself to the waist. Then the water was too muddy to admit of his seeing the fish, and he was compelled to wait until the sediment had settled.

The pursuit was renewed, till the water was again muddied. But he could not wait. He unstrapped the tin bucket and began to bail the pool. He bailed wildly at first, splashing himself and flinging the water so short a distance that it ran back into the pool. He worked more carefully, striving to be cool, though his heart was pounding against his chest and his hands were trembling. At the end of half an hour the pool was nearly dry. Not a cupful of water remained. And there was no fish. He found a hidden crevice among the stones through which it had escaped to the adjoining and larger pool—a pool which he could not empty in a night and a day. Had he known of the crevice, he could have closed it with a rock at the beginning and the fish would have been his.

Thus he thought, and crumpled up and sank down upon the wet earth. At first he cried softly to himself, then he cried loudly to the pitiless desolation that ringed him around, and for a long time after he was shaken by great dry sobs.

He built a fire and warmed himself by drinking quarts of hot water, and made camp on a rocky ledge in the same fashion he had the night before. The last thing he did was to see that his matches were dry and to wind his watch. The

blankets were wet and clammy. His ankle pulsed with pain.
But he knew only that he was hungry, and through his restless
sleep he dreamed of feasts and banquets and of food served and
spread in all imaginable ways.

He awoke chilled and sick. There was no sun. The grey of
earth and sky had become deeper, more profound. A raw
wind was blowing, and the first flurries of snow were whitening
the hilltops. The air about him thickened and grew white
while he made a fire and boiled more water. It was wet snow,
half rain, and the flakes were large and soggy. At first they
melted as soon as they came in contact with the earth, but
ever more fell, covering the ground, putting out the fire,
spoiling his supply of moss fuel.

This was a signal for him to strap on his pack and stumble
onward, he knew not where. He was not concerned with the
land of little sticks, nor with Bill and the cache under the upturned canoe by the river Dease. He was mastered by the verb
'to eat'. He was hunger-mad. He took no heed of the course
he pursued, so long as that course led him through the swale
bottoms. He felt his way through the wet snow to the watery
muskeg berries, and went by feel as he pulled up the rush
grass by the roots. But it was tasteless stuff and did not satisfy.
He found a weed that tasted sour and he ate all he could
find of it, which was not much, for it was a creeping growth,
easily hidden under the several inches of snow.

He had no fire that night, nor hot water, and crawled under
his blanket to sleep the broken hunger sleep. The snow turned
into a cold rain. He awakened many times to feel it falling on
his upturned face. Day came—a grey day and no sun. It had
ceased raining. The keenness of his hunger had departed.
Sensibility, as far as concerned the yearning for food, had been
exhausted. There was a dull, heavy ache in his stomach, but
it did not bother him so much. He was more rational, and once
more he was chiefly interested in the land of little sticks and
the cache by the river Dease.

He ripped the remnant of one of his blankets into strips and
bound his bleeding feet. Also he recinched the injured ankle

and prepared himself for a day of travel. When he came to his pack he paused long over the squat moose-hide sack, but in the end it went with him.

The snow had melted under the rain, and only the hilltops showed white. The sun came out, and he succeeded in locating the points of the compass, though he knew now that he was lost. Perhaps, in his previous days' wanderings, he had edged away too far to the left. He now bore off to the right to counteract the possible deviation from his true course.

Though the hunger pangs were no longer so exquisite, he realized that he was weak. He was compelled to pause for frequent rests, when he attacked the muskeg berries and rushgrass patches. His tongue felt dry and large, as though covered with a fine hairy growth, and it tasted bitter in his mouth. His heart gave him a great deal of trouble. When he had travelled a few minutes it would begin a remorseless thump, thump, thump, and then leap up and away in a painful flutter of beats that choked him and made him go faint and dizzy.

In the middle of the day he found two minnows in a large pool. It was impossible to bail it, but he was calmer now and managed to catch them in his tin bucket. They were no longer than his little finger, but he was not particularly hungry. The dull ache in his stomach had been growing duller and fainter. It seemed almost that his stomach was dozing. He ate the fish raw, masticating with painstaking care, for the eating was an act of pure reason. While he had no desire to eat, he knew that he must eat to live.

In the evening he caught three more minnows, eating two and saving the third for breakfast. The sun had dried stray shreds of moss, and he was able to warm himself with hot water. He had not covered more than ten miles that day; and the next day, travelling whenever his heart permitted him, he covered no more than five miles. But his stomach did not give him the slightest uneasiness. It had gone to sleep. He was in a strange country, too, and the caribou were growing more plentiful, also the wolves. Often their yelps drifted across the desolation, and once he saw three of them slinking away before his path.

Another night; and in the morning, being more rational, he untied the leather string that fastened the squat moose-hide sack. From its open mouth poured a yellow stream of coarse gold dust and nuggets. He roughly divided the gold in halves, caching one half on a prominent ledge, wrapped in a piece of blanket, and returning the other half to the sack. He also began to use strips of the one remaining blanket for his feet. He still clung to his gun, for there were cartridges in that cache by the river Dease.

This was a day of fog, and this day hunger awoke in him again. He was very weak and was afflicted with a giddiness which at times blinded him. It was no uncommon thing now for him to stumble and fall; and stumbling once, he fell squarely into a ptarmigan nest. There were four newly hatched chicks, a day old—little specks of pulsating life no more than a mouthful; and he ate them ravenously, thrusting them alive into his mouth and crunching them like eggshells between his teeth. The mother ptarmigan beat about him with great outcry. He used his gun as a club with which to knock her over, but she dodged out of reach. He threw stones at her and with one chance shot broke a wing. Then she fluttered away, running, trailing the broken wing, with him in pursuit.

The little chicks had no more than whetted his appetite. He hopped and bobbed clumsily along on his injured ankle, throwing stones and screaming hoarsely at times; at other times hopping and bobbing silently along, picking himself up grimly and patiently when he fell, or rubbing his eyes with his hand when the giddiness threatened to overpower him.

The chase led him across swampy ground in the bottom of the valley, and he came upon footprints in the soggy moss. They were not his own—he could see that. They must be Bill's. But he could not stop, for the mother ptarmigan was running on. He would catch her first, then he would return and investigate.

He exhausted the mother ptarmigan; but he exhausted himself. She lay panting on her side. He lay panting on his side, a dozen feet away, unable to crawl to her. And as he recovered she recovered, fluttering out of reach as his hungry hand went out to her. The chase was resumed. Night settled down and she escaped. He stumbled from weakness and pitched head foremost on his face, cutting his cheek, his pack upon his back. He did not move for a long while; then he rolled over on his side, wound his watch, and lay there until morning.

Another day of fog. Half of his last blanket had gone into foot-wrappings. He failed to pick up Bill's trail. It did not matter. His hunger was driving him too compellingly—only—only he wondered if Bill, too, were lost. By midday the irk of his pack became too oppressive. Again he divided the gold, this time merely spilling half of it on the ground. In the after-noon he threw the rest of it away, there remaining to him only the half blanket, the tin bucket, and the rifle.

A hallucination began to trouble him. He felt confident that one cartridge remained to him. It was in the chamber of the rifle and he had overlooked it. On the other hand, he knew all the time that the chamber was empty. But the hallucination persisted. He fought it off for hours, then threw his rifle open and was confronted with emptiness. The disappointment was as bitter as though he had really expected to find the cartridge.

He plodded on for half an hour, when the hallucination arose again. Again he fought it, and still it persisted, till for very relief he opened his rifle to unconvince himself. At times his mind wandered further afield, and he plodded on, a mere automaton, strange conceits and whimsicalities gnawing at his brain like worms. But these excursions out of the real were of brief duration, for ever the pangs of the hunger bite called him back. He was jerked back abruptly once from such an excursion by a sight that caused him nearly to faint. He reeled and swayed, doddering like a drunken man to keep from falling. Before him stood a horse. A horse! He could not believe his eyes. A thick mist was in them, intershot with sparkling points of light. He rubbed his eyes savagely to clear his vision, and beheld not a horse but a great brown bear. The animal was studying him with bellicose curiosity.

The man had brought his gun half-way to his shoulder before he realized. He lowered it and drew his hunting knife from its beaded sheath at his hip. Before him was meat and life. He ran his thumb along the edge of his knife. It was sharp. The point was sharp. He would fling himself upon the bear and kill it. But his heart began its warning thump, thump, thump. Then followed the wild upward leap and tattoo of flutters, the pressings as of an iron band about his forehead, the creeping of the dizziness into his brain.

His desperate courage was evicted by a great surge of fear. In his weakness, what if the animal attacked him? He drew himself up to his most imposing stature, gripping the knife and staring hard at the bear. The bear advanced clumsily a couple of steps, reared up, and gave vent to a tentative growl. If the man ran, he would run after him; but the man did not run. He was animated now with the courage of fear. He, too, growled, savagely, terribly, voicing the fear that is to life germane and that lies twisted about life's deepest roots.

The bear edged away to one side, growling menacingly, himself appalled by this mysterious creature that appeared upright and unafraid. But the man did not move. He stood like a statue till the danger was past, when he yielded to a fit of trembling and sank down into the wet moss.

He pulled himself together and went on, afraid now in a new way. It was not the fear that he should die passively from lack of food, but that he should be destroyed violently before starvation had exhausted the last particle of the endeavour in him that made towards surviving. There were the wolves. Back and forth across the desolation drifted their howls, weaving the very air into a fabric of menace that was so tangible that he found himself, arms in the air, pressing it back from him as it might be the walls of a wind-blown tent.

Now and again the wolves, in packs of two and three, crossed his path. But they sheered clear of him. They were not in sufficient numbers, and besides, they were hunting the caribou, which did not battle, while this strange creature that walked erect might scratch and bite.

In the late afternoon he came upon scattered bones where the wolves had made a kill. The debris had been a caribou calf an hour before, squawking and running and very much alive. He contemplated the bones, clean-picked and polished, pink with the cell life in them which had not yet died. Could it possibly be that he might be that ere the day was done! Such was life, eh? A vain and fleeting thing. It was only life that pained. There was no hurt in death. To die was to sleep. It meant cessation, rest. Then why was he not content to die?

But he did not moralize long. He was squatting in the moss, a bone in his mouth, sucking at the shreds of life that still dyed it faintly pink. The sweet meaty taste, thin and elusive, almost as a memory, maddened him. He closed his jaws on the bones and crunched. Sometimes it was the bone that broke sometimes his teeth. Then he crushed the bones between rocks, pounded them to a pulp, and swallowed them. He pounded his fingers, too, in his haste, and yet found a moment in which to feel surprise at the fact that his fingers did not hurt much when caught under the descending rock.

Came frightful days of snow and rain. He did not know when he made camp, when he broke camp. He travelled in the night as much as in the day. He rested wherever he fell, crawled on whenever the dying life in him flickered up and burned less dimly. He, as a man, no longer strove. It was the life in him, unwilling to die, that drove him on. He did not suffer. His nerves had become blunted, numb, while his mind was filled with weird visions and delicious dreams.

But ever he sucked and chewed on the crushed bones of the caribou calf, the least remnants of which he had gathered up and carried with him. He crossed no more hills or divides, but automatically followed a large stream which flowed through a wide and shallow valley. He did not see this stream nor this valley. He saw nothing save visions. Soul and body walked or crawled side by side, yet apart, so slender was the thread that bound them.

He awoke in his right mind, lying on his back on a rocky ledge. The sun was shining bright and warm. Afar off he heard the squawking of caribou calves. He was aware of vague memories of rain and wind and snow, but whether he had been beaten by the storm for two days or two weeks he did not know.

For some time he lay without movement, the genial sunshine pouring upon him and saturating his miserable body with its warmth. A fine day, he thought. Perhaps he could manage to locate himself. By a painful effort he rolled over on his side. Below him flowed a wide and sluggish river. Its unfamiliarity puzzled him. Slowly he followed it with his eyes, winding in wide sweeps among the bleak, bare hills, bleaker and barer and lower-lying than any hills he had yet encountered. Slowly, deliberately, without excitement or more than the most casual interest, he followed the course of the strange stream towards the skyline and saw it emptying into a bright and shining sea. He was still unexcited. Most unusual, he thought, a vision or a mirage—more likely a vision, a trick of his disordered mind. He was confirmed in this by sight of a ship lying at anchor in the midst of the shining sea. He closed his eyes for a while, then opened them. Strange how the vision persisted! Yet not strange. He knew there were no seas or ships in the heart of the barren lands, just as he had known there was no cartridge in the empty rifle.

He heard a snuffle behind him—a half-choking gasp or cough. Very slowly, because of his exceeding weakness and stiffness, he rolled over on his other side. He could see nothing near at hand, but he waited patiently. Again came the snuffle and cough, and outlined between two jagged rocks not a score of feet away he made out the grey head of a wolf. The sharp ears were not pricked so sharply as he had seen them on other wolves; the eyes were bleared and bloodshot, the head seemed to droop limply and forlornly. The animal blinked continually in the sunshine. It seemed sick. As he looked it snuffed and coughed again.

This, at least, was real, he thought, and turned on the other side so that he might see the reality of the world which had been veiled from him before by the vision. But the sea still shone in the distance and the ship was plainly discernible. Was it reality after all? He closed his eyes for a long while and thought, and then it came to him. He had been making north by east, away from the Dease Divide and into the Coppermine Valley. This wide and sluggish river was the Coppermine. That shining sea was the Arctic Ocean. That ship was a whaler, strayed east, far east, from the mouth of the Mackenzie and it was lying at anchor in Coronation Gulf. He remembered the Hudson's Bay Company chart he had seen long ago, and it was all clear and reasonable to him.

He sat up and turned his attention to immediate affairs. He had worn through the blanket wrappings, and his feet were shapeless lumps of raw meat. His last blanket was gone. Rifle and knife were both missing. He had lost his hat somewhere, with the bunch of matches in the band, but the matches against his chest were safe and dry inside the tobacco pouch and oil paper. He looked at his watch. It marked eleven o'clock and was still running. Evidently he had kept it wound.

He was calm and collected. Though extremely weak, he had no sensation of pain. He was not hungry. The thought of food was not even pleasant to him, and whatever he did was done by his reason alone. He ripped off his pants' legs to the knees and bound them about his feet. Somehow he had succeeded in retaining the tin bucket. He would have some hot water before he began what he foresaw was to be a terrible journey to the ship.

His movements were slow. He shook as with a palsy. When he started to collect dry moss he found he could not rise to his feet. He tried again and again, then contented himself with crawling about on hands and knees. Once he crawled near to the sick wolf. The animal dragged itself reluctantly out of his way, licking its chops with a tongue which seemed hardly to have the strength to curl. The man noticed that the tongue was not the customary healthful red. It was a yellowish brown and seemed coated with a rough and half-dry mucus.

After he had drunk a quart of hot water the man found he

was able to stand, and even walk as well as a dying man might be supposed to walk. Every minute or so he was compelled to rest. His steps were feeble and uncertain, just as the wolf's that trailed him were feeble and uncertain; and that night, when the shining sea was blotted out by blackness, he knew he was nearer to it by no more than four miles.

Throughout the night he heard the cough of the sick wolf, and now and then the squawking of the caribou calves. There was life all around him, but it was strong life, very much alive and well, and he knew the sick wolf clung to the sick man's trail in the hope that the man would die first. In the morning, on opening his eyes, he beheld it regarding him with a wistful and hungry stare. It stood crouched, with tail between its legs, like a miserable and woebegone dog. It shivered in the chill morning wind and grinned dispiritedly when the man spoke to it in a voice that achieved no more than a hoarse whisper.

The sun rose brightly, and all morning the man tottered and fell towards the ship on the shining sea. The weather was perfect. It was the brief Indian summer of the high latitudes. It might last a week. Tomorrow or next day it might be gone.

In the afternoon the man came upon a trail. It was of another man, who did not walk, but who dragged himself on all fours. The man thought it might be Bill, but he thought in a dull, uninterested way. He had no curiosity. In fact sensation and emotion had left him. He was no longer susceptible to pain, Stomach and nerves had gone to sleep. Yet the life that was in him drove him on. He was very weary, but it refused to die. It was because it refused to die that he still ate muskeg berries and minnows, drank his hot water, and kept a wary eye on the sick wolf.

He followed the trail of the other man who dragged himself along, and soon came to the end of it—a few fresh-picked bones where the soggy moss was marked by the foot pads of many wolves. He saw a squat moose-hide sack, mate to his own, which had been torn by sharp teeth. He picked it up, though its weight was almost too much for his feeble fingers. Bill had carried it to the last. Ha-ha! He would have the laugh on Bill.

He would survive and carry it to the ship in the shining sea. His mirth was hoarse and ghastly, like a raven's croak, and the sick wolf joined him, howling lugubriously. The man ceased suddenly. How could he have the laugh on Bill if that were Bill; if those bones, so pinky-white and clean, were Bill?

He turned away. Well, Bill had deserted him; but he would not take the gold, nor would he suck Bill's bones. Bill would have, though, had it been the other way round, he mused as he staggered on.

He came to a pool of water. Stooping over in quest of minnows, he jerked his head back as though he had been stung. He had caught sight of his reflected face. So horrible was it that sensibility awoke long enough to be shocked. There were three minnows in the pool, which was too large to drain; and after several ineffectual attempts to catch them in the tin bucket he forbore. He was afraid, because of his great weakness, that he might fall in and drown. It was for this reason that he did not trust himself to the river astride one of the many drift logs which lined its sandpits.

That day he decreased the distance between him and the ship by three miles; the next day by two—for he was crawling now as Bill had crawled; and the end of the fifth day found the ship still seven miles away and him unable to make even a mile a day. Still the Indian summer held on, and he continued to crawl and faint, turn and turn about; and ever the sick wolf coughed and wheezed at his heels. His knees had become raw meat like his feet, and though he padded them with the shirt from his back it was a red track he left behind him on the moss and stones. Once, glancing back, he saw the wolf licking hungrily his bleeding trail, and he saw sharply what his own end might be—unless—unless he could get the wolf. Then began as grim a tragedy of existence as was ever played—a sick man that crawled, a sick wolf that limped, two creatures dragging their dying carcasses across the desolation and hunting each other's lives.

Had it been a well wolf, it would not have mattered so much to the man; but the thought of going to feed the maw of that loathsome and all but dead thing was repugnant to him. He was finicky. His mind had begun to wander again and to be perplexed by hallucinations, while his lucid intervals grew rarer and shorter.

He was awakened once from a faint by a wheeze close in his ear. The wolf leaped lamely back, losing its footing and falling in its weakness. It was ludicrous, but he was not amused. Nor was he even afraid. He was too far gone for that. But his mind was for the moment clear, and he lay and considered. The ship was no more than four miles away. He could see it quite distinctly when he rubbed the mists out of his eyes, and he could see the white sail of a small boat cutting the water of the shining sea. But he could never crawl those four miles. He knew that, and was very calm in the knowledge. He knew that he could not crawl half a mile. And yet he wanted to live. It was unreasonable that he should die after all he had undergone. Fate asked too much of him. And, dying, he declined to die. It was stark madness, perhaps, but in the very grip of death he defied death and refused to die.

He closed his eyes and composed himself with infinite precaution. He steeled himself to keep above the suffocating languor that lapped like a rising tide through all the wells of his being. It was very like a sea, this deadly languor that rose and drowned his consciousness bit by bit. Sometimes he was all but submerged, swimming through oblivion with a faltering stroke; and again, by some strange alchemy of soul, he would find another shred of will and strike out more strongly.

Without movement he lay on his back, and he could hear, slowly drawing nearer and nearer, the wheezing intake and output of the sick wolf's breath. It drew closer, ever closer, through an infinitude of time, and he did not move. It was at his ear. The harsh dry tongue grated like sandpaper against his cheek. His hand shot out—or at least he willed them to shoot out. The fingers were curved like talons, but they closed on empty air. Swiftness and certitude require strength, and the man had not this strength.

The patience of the wolf was terrible. The man's patience

was no less terrible. For half a day he lay motionless, fighting off unconsciousness and waiting for the thing that was to feed upon him and upon which he wished to feed. Sometimes the languid sea rose over him and he dreamed long dreams; but ever through it all, waking and dreaming, he waited for the wheezing breath and the harsh caress of the tongue.

He did not hear the breath, and he slipped slowly from some dream to the feel of the tongue along his hand. He waited. The fangs pressed softly; the pressure increased; the wolf was exerting its last strength in an effort to sink teeth in the food for which it had waited so long. But the man had waited long, and the lacerated hand closed on the jaw. Slowly, while the wolf struggled feebly and the hand clutched feebly, the other hand crept across to a grip. Five minutes later the whole weight of the man's body was on top of the wolf. The hands had not sufficient strength to choke the wolf, but the face of the man was pressed close to the throat of the wolf and the mouth of the man was full of hair. At the end of half an hour the man was aware of a warm trickle in his throat. It was not pleasant. It was like molten lead being forced into his stomach, and it was forced by his will alone. Later on the man rolled over on his back and slept.

There were some members of a scientific expedition on the whaleship *Bedford*. From the deck they remarked a strange object on the shore. It was moving down the beach towards the water. They were unable to classify it, and, being scientific men, they climbed into the whaleboat alongside and went ashore to see. And they saw something that was alive but which could hardly be called a man. It was blind, unconscious. It squirmed along the ground like some monstrous worm. Most of its efforts were ineffectual, but it was persistent, and it writhed and twisted and went ahead perhaps a score of feet an hour.

Three weeks afterwards the man lay in a bunk on the whaleship *Bedford*, and with tears streaming down his wasted cheeks told who he was and what he had undergone. He also babbled incoherently of his mother, of sunny southern California, and a home among the orange groves and flowers.

The days were not many after that when he sat at table with the scientific men and the ship's officers. He gloated over the spectacle of so much food, watching it anxiously as it went into the mouths of others. With the disappearance of each mouthful an expression of deep regret came into his eyes. He was quite sane, yet he hated those men at mealtime. He was haunted by a fear that the food would not last. He inquired of the cook, the cabin boy, the captain, concerning the food stores. They reassured him countless times; but he could not believe them, and pried cunningly about the lazaret to see with his own eyes.

It was noticed that the man was getting fat. He grew stouter with each day. The scientific men shook their heads and theorized. They limited the man at his meals, but still his girth increased and he swelled prodigiously under his shirt.

The sailors grinned. They knew. And when the scientific men set a watch on the man they knew. They saw him slouch for'ard after breakfast, and, like a mendicant, with out-stretched palm, accost a sailor. The sailor grinned and passed him a fragment of sea biscuit. He clutched it avariciously, looked at it as a miser looks at gold, and thrust it into his shirt bosom. Similar were the donations from other grinning sailors.

The scientific men were discreet. They let him alone. But they privily examined his bunk. It was lined with hardtack; the mattress was stuffed with hardtack; every nook and cranny was filled with hardtack. Yet he was sane. He was taking precautions against another possible famine—that was all. He would recover from it, the scientific men said; and he did, ere the *Bedford*'s anchor rumbled down in San Francisco Bay.

C

To the Man on Trail

'DUMP it in.'

'But I say, Kid, isn't that going a little too strong? Whisky and alcohol's bad enough; but when it comes to brandy and pepper-sauce and——'

'Dump it in. Who's making this punch, anyway?' And Malemute Kid smiled benignantly through the clouds of steam. 'By the time you've been in this country as long as I have, my son, and lived on rabbit-tracks and salmon belly, you'll learn that Christmas comes only once per annum. And a Christmas without punch is sinking a hole to bedrock with nary a pay-streak.'

'Stack up on that fer a high cyard,' approved Big Jim Belden, who had come down from his claim on Mazy May to spend Christmas, and who, as everyone knew, had been living the two months past on straight moose-meat. 'Hain't fergot the *hooch* we-uns made on the Tanana, hev yeh?'

'Well, I guess yes. Boys, it would have done your hearts good to see that whole tribe fighting drunk—and all because of a glorious ferment of sugar and sour dough. That was before your time,' Malemute Kid said as he turned to Stanley Prince, a young mining expert who had been in two years. 'No white women in the country then, and Mason wanted to get married. Ruth's father was chief of the Tananas, and objected, like the rest of the tribe. Stiff? Why, I used my last pound of sugar; finest work in that line I ever did in my life. You should have seen the chase, down the river and across the portage.'

'But the squaw?' asked Louis Savoy, the tall French-Canadian, becoming interested; for he had heard of this wild deed, when at Forty-Mile the preceding winter.

Then Malemute Kid, who was a born raconteur, told the unvarnished tale of the Northland Lochinvar. More than one rough adventurer of the north felt his heartstrings draw closer, and experienced vague yearnings for the sunnier pastures of the Southland, where life promised something more than a barren struggle with cold and death.

'We struck the Yukon just behind the first ice-run,' he concluded, 'and the tribe only a quarter of an hour behind. But that saved us; for the second run broke the jam above, and shut them out. When they finally got into Nuklukyeto, the whole Post was ready for them. And as to the foregathering, ask Father Roubeau here: he performed the ceremony.'

The Jesuit took the pipe from his lips, but could only express his gratification with patriarchal smiles, while Protestant and Catholic vigorously applauded.

'By gar!' ejaculated Louis Savoy, who seemed overcome by the romance of it. '*La petite squaw; mon Mason brav.* By gar!'

Then, as the first tin cups of punch went round, Bettles the Unquenchable sprang to his feet and struck up his favourite drinking song:

> 'There's Henry Ward Beecher
> And Sunday School teachers,
>   All drink of the sassafras root;
> But you bet all the same,
> If it had its right name,
>   It's the juice of the forbidden fruit.'

> 'Oh, the juice of the forbidden fruit,'

roared out the Bacchanalian chorus:

> 'Oh the juice of the forbidden fruit;
>   But you bet all the same,
>   If it had its right name,
> It's the juice of the forbidden fruit.'

Malemute Kid's frightful concoction did its work; the men of the camps and trails unbent in its genial glow, and jest and song and tales of past adventure went round and board. Aliens from a dozen lands, they toasted each and all. It was the Englishman, Prince, who pledged 'Uncle Sam, the precocious infant of the New World'; the Yankee, Bettles, who drank to 'The Queen, God bless her'; and together, Savoy and Meyers, the German trader, clanged their cups to Alsace and Lorraine.

Then Malemute Kid arose, cup in hand, and glanced at the greased-paper window, where the frost stood full three inches thick. 'A health to the man on trail this night; may his grub hold out; may his dogs keep their legs; may his matches never miss fire.'

Crack! Crack!—they heard the familiar music of the dog-whip, the whining howl of the Malemutes, and the crunch of a sled as it drew up to the cabin. Conversation languished while they waited the issue.

'An old-timer; cares for his dogs and then himself,' whispered Malemute Kid to Prince, as they listened to the snapping jaws and the wolfish snarls and yelps of pain which proclaimed to their practised ears that the stranger was beating back their dogs while he fed his own.

Then came the expected knock, sharp and confident, and the stranger entered. Dazzled by the light, he hesitated a moment at the door, giving to all a chance for scrutiny. He was a striking personage, and a most picturesque one, in his Arctic dress of wool and fur. Standing six foot two or three, with proportionate breadth of shoulders and depth of chest, his smooth-shaven face nipped by the cold to a gleaming pink, his long lashes and eyebrows white with ice, and the ear and neck flaps of his great wolfskin cap loosely raised, he seemed, of a verity, the frost king, just stepped in out of the night. Clasped outside his mackinaw jacket, a beaded belt held two large Colt's revolvers and a hunting-knife, while he carried, in addition to the inevitable dogwhip, a smokeless rifle of the largest bore and latest pattern. As he came forward, for all his step was firm and elastic, they could see that fatigue bore heavily upon him.

An awkward silence had fallen, but his hearty 'What cheer, my lads?' put them quickly at ease, and the next instant Malemute Kid and he had gripped hands. Though they had never met, each had heard of the other, and the recognition was mutual. A sweeping introduction and a mug of punch were forced upon him before he could explain his errand.

'How long since that basket-sled, with three men and eight dogs passed?' he asked.

'An even two days ahead. Are you after them?'

'Yes; my team. Run them off under my very nose, the cusses. I've gained two days on them already—pick them up on the next run.'

'Reckon they'll show spunk?' asked Belden, in order to keep up the conversation, for Malemute Kid already had the coffee-pot on, and was busily frying bacon and moose-meat.

The stranger significantly tapped his revolvers.

'When'd yeh leave Dawson?'

'Last night?'—as a matter of course.

'Today.'

A murmur of surprise passed round the circle. And well it might; for it was just midnight, and seventy-five miles of rough river trail was not to be sneered at for a twelve hours' run.

The talk soon became impersonal, however, harking back to the trails of childhood. As the young stranger ate of the rude fare, Malemute Kid attentively studied his face. Nor was he long in deciding that it was fair, honest and open, and that he liked it. Still youthful, the lines had been firmly traced by toil and hardship. Though genial in conversation, and mild when at rest, the blue eyes gave promise of the hard steel-glitter which comes when called into action, especially against odds. The heavy jaw and square-cut chin demonstrated rugged pertinacity and indomitability. Nor, though the attributes of the lion were there, was there wanting the certain softness, the hint of womanliness, which bespoke the emotional nature.

'So, thet's how me an' the ol' woman got spliced,' said Belden, concluding the exciting tale of his courtship. '"Here we be, dad," sez she. "An' may yeh be damned," sez he to her, an' then to me, "Jim, yeh—yeh git outen them good duds o' yourn; I want a right peart slice o' thet forty acre ploughed 'fore dinner." An' then he turns on her an' sez, "An' yeh, Sal; yeh sail inter them dishes." An' I was thet happy—but he seen me an roars out, "Yeh, Jim!" An' yeh bet I dusted for the barn.'

'Any kids waiting for you back in the States?' asked the stranger.

'Nope; Sal died 'fore any come. Thet's why I'm here.' Belden abstractedly began to light his pipe, which had failed to go out, and then brightened up with, 'How 'bout yerself, stranger—married man?'

For reply, he opened his watch, slipped it from the thong which served for a chain, and passed it over. Belden picked up the slush-lamp, surveyed the inside of the case critically, and swearing admiringly to himself, handed it over to Louis Savoy. With numerous 'By gars!' he finally surrendered it to Prince, and they noticed that his hands trembled and his eyes took on a peculiar softness. And so it passed from horny hand to horny hand—the pasted photograph of a woman, the clinging kind that such men fancy, with a babe at the breast. Those who had not yet seen the wonder were keen with curiosity; those who had, became silent and retrospective. They could face the pinch of famine, the grip of scurvy, or the quick death by field or flood; but the pictured semblance of a stranger woman and child made women and children of them all.

'Never have seen the youngster yet—he's a boy, she says, and two years old,' said the stranger as he received the treasure back. A lingering moment he gazed upon it, then snapped the case and turned away, but not quick enough to hide the restrained rush of tears.

Malemute Kid led him to a bunk and bade him turn in.

'Call me at four, sharp. Don't fail me,' were his last words, and a moment later he was breathing in the heaviness of exhausted sleep.

'By Jove! he's a plucky chap,' commented Prince. 'Three hours' sleep after seventy-five miles with the dogs, and then the trail again. Who is he, Kid?'

'Jack Westondale. Been in going on three years, with nothing but the name of working like a horse, and any amount of bad luck to his credit. I never knew him, but Sitka Charley told me about him.'

'It seems hard that a man with a sweet young wife like his should be putting in his years in this God-forsaken hole, where every year counts two on the outside.'

'The trouble with him is clean grit and stubbornness. He's cleaned up twice with a stake, but lost it both times.'

Here the conversation was broken off by an uproar from Bettles, for the effect had begun to wear away. And soon the bleak years of monotonous grub and deadening toil were being forgotten in rough merriment. Malemute Kid alone seemed unable to lose himself, and cast many an anxious look at his watch. Once he put on his mittens and beaver-skin cap, and leaving the cabin, fell to rummaging about in the cache.

Nor could he wait the hour designated; for he was fifteen minutes ahead of time in rousing his guest. The young giant had stiffened badly, and brisk rubbing was necessary to bring him to his feet. He tottered painfully out of the cabin, to find his dogs harnessed and everything ready for the start. The company wished him good luck and a short chase, while Father Roubeau, hurriedly blessing him, led the stampede for the cabin; and small wonder, for it is not good to face seventy-four degrees below zero with naked ears and hands.

Malemute Kid saw him to the main trail, and there, gripping his hand heartily, gave him advice.

'You'll find a hundred pounds of salmon-eggs on the sled,' he said. 'The dogs will go as far on that as with one hundred and fifty of fish, and you can't get dog-food at Pelly, as you probably expected.' The stranger started, and his eyes flashed, but he did not interrupt. 'You can't get an ounce of food for dog or man till you reach Five Fingers, and that's a stiff two hundred miles. Watch out for open water on the Thirty Mile River, and be sure you take the big cut-off above Le Barge.'

'How did you know it? Surely the news can't be ahead of me already?'

'I don't know it; and what's more, I don't want to know it. But you never owned that team you're chasing. Sitka Charley sold it to them last spring. But he sized you up to me as square once, and I believe him. I've seen your face; I like it. And I've seen—why, damn you, hit the high places for salt water and that wife of yours and——' Here the Kid unmittened and jerked out his sack.

'No; I don't need it,' and the tears froze on his cheeks as he convulsively gripped Malemute Kid's hand.

'Then don't spare the dogs; cut them out of the traces as fast as they drop; buy them, and think they're cheap at ten dollars a pound. You can get them at Five Fingers, Little Salmon, and the Hootalinqua. And watch out for wet feet,' was his parting advice. 'Keep a-travelling up to twenty-five, but if it gets below that, build a fire and change your socks.'

Fifteen minutes had barely elapsed when the jingle of bells announced new arrivals. The door opened, and a mounted policeman of the North-west Territory entered, followed by two half-breed dog-drivers. Like Westondale, they were heavily armed, and showed signs of fatigue. The half-breeds had been born to the trail, and bore it easily; but the young policeman was badly exhausted. Still, the dogged obstinacy of his race held him to the pace he had set, and would hold him till he dropped in his tracks.

'When did Westondale pull out?' he asked. 'He stopped here, didn't he?' This was supererogatory, for the tracks told their own tale too well.

Malemute Kid had caught Belden's eye, and he, scenting the wind, replied evasively, 'A right peart while back.'

'Come, my man; speak up,' the policeman admonished.

'Yeh seem to want him right smart. Hez he ben gittin' cantankerous down Dawson way?'

'Held up Harry McFarland's for forty thousand; exchanged

it at the P.C. store for a cheque on Seattle; and who's to stop the cashing of it if we don't overtake him? When did he pull out?'

Every eye suppressed its excitement, for Malemute Kid had given the cue, and the young officer encountered wooden faces on every hand.

Striding over to Prince, he put his question to him. Though it hurt him, gazing into the frank, earnest face of his fellow countryman, he replied inconsequentially on the state of the trail.

Then he espied Father Roubeau, who could not lie. 'A quarter of an hour ago,' the priest answered; 'but he had three hours' rest for himself and dogs.'

'Fifteen minutes' start, and he's fresh! My God!' The poor fellow staggered back, half fainting from exhaustion and disappointment, murmuring something about the run from Dawson in ten hours, and the dogs being played out.

Malemute Kid forced a mug of punch upon him; then he turned for the door, ordering the dog-drivers to follow. But the warmth and promise of rest were too tempting, and they objected strenuously. The Kid was conversant with their French patois, and followed it anxiously.

They swore that the dogs were done up; that Siwash and Babette would have to be shot before the first mile was covered; that the rest were almost as bad; and that it would be better for all hands to rest up.

'Lend me five dogs?' he asked, turning to Malemute Kid.

But the Kid shook his head.

'I'll sign a cheque on Captain Constantine for five thousand —here's my papers—I'm authorized to draw at my own discretion.'

Again the silent refusal.

'Then I'll requisition them in the name of the Queen.'

Smiling incredulously, the Kid glanced at his well-stocked arsenal, and the Englishman, realizing his impotency, turned for the door. But the dog-drivers still objecting, he whirled upon them fiercely, calling them women and curs. The swart face of the older half-breed flushed angrily, as he drew himself up and promised in good round terms that he would travel his leader off his legs, and would then be delighted to plant him in the snow.

The young officer—and it required his whole will—walked steadily to the door, exhibiting a freshness he did not possess. But they all knew, and appreciated his proud effort; nor could he veil the twinges of agony that shot across his face. Covered with frost, the dogs were curled up in the snow, and it was almost impossible to get them to their feet. The poor brutes whined under the stinging lash, for the dog-drivers were angry and cruel; nor till Babette, the leader was cut from the traces, could they break out the sled and get under way.

'A dirty scoundrel and a liar!' 'By gar! him no good!' 'A thief!' 'Worse than an Indian!' It was evident that they were angry—first, at the way they had been deceived; and second, at the outraged ethics of the Northland, where honesty, above all, was man's prime jewel. 'An' we gave the cuss a hand, after knowin' what he'd did.' All eyes were turned accusingly upon Malemute Kid, who rose from the corner where he had been making Babette comfortable, and silently emptied the bowl for a final round of punch.

'It's a cold night, boys—a bitter cold night,' was the irrelevant commencement of his defence. 'You've all travelled trail, and know what that stands for. Don't jump a dog when he's down. You've only heard one side. A whiter man than Jack Westondale never ate from the same pot nor stretched blanket with you or me. Last fall he gave his whole clean-up, forty thousand, to Joe Castrell, to buy in on Dominion. Today he'd be a millionaire. But while he stayed behind at Circle City, taking care of his partner with the scurvy, what does Castrell do? Goes into McFarland's, jumps the limit, and drops the whole sack. Found him dead in the snow the next day. And poor Jack laying his plans to go out this winter to his wife and the boy he's never seen. You'll notice he took exactly what his partner lost—forty thousand. Well, he's gone out; and what are you going to do about it?'

The Kid glanced round the circle of his judges, noted the softening of their faces, then raised his mug aloft. 'So a health to the man on trail this night; may his grub hold out; may his dogs keep their legs; may his matches never miss fire. God prosper him; good luck go with him; and——'

'Confusion to the mounted police!' cried Bettles, to the crash of the empty cups.

The Heathen

I MET him first in a hurricane; and though we had gone
through the hurricane on the same schooner, it was not
until the schooner had gone to pieces under us that I first laid
eyes on him. Without doubt I had seen him with the rest of
the Kanaka crew on board, but I had not consciously been
aware of his existence, for the *Petite Jeanne* was rather over-
crowded. In addition to her eight or ten Kanaka seamen, her
white captain, mate, and supercargo, and her six cabin
passengers, she sailed from Rangiroa with something like
eighty-five deck passengers—Paumotans and Tahitians, men,
women, and children each with a trade box, to say nothing of
sleeping-mats, blankets, and clothes bundles.

The pearling season in the Paumotas was over, and all hands
were returning to Tahiti. The six of us cabin passengers were
pearl buyers. Two were Americans, one was Ah Choon (the
whitest Chinese I have ever known), one was a German, one
was a Polish Jew, and I completed the half-dozen.

It had been a prosperous season. Not one of us had cause for
complaint, nor one of the eighty-five deck passengers either.
All had done well, and all were looking forward to a rest-off
and a good time in Papeete.

Of course the *Petite Jeanne* was overloaded. She was only
seventy tons, and she had no right to carry a tithe of the mob
she had on board. Beneath her hatches she was crammed and
jammed with pearl shell and copra. Even the trade room was
packed full with shell. It was a miracle that the sailors could
work her. There was no moving about the decks. They simply
climbed back and forth along the rails.

In the night-time they walked upon the sleepers, who
carpeted the deck, I'll swear, two deep. Oh, and there were
pigs and chickens on deck, and sacks of yams, while every
conceivable place was festooned with strings of drinking coconuts and bunches of bananas. On both sides, between the fore
and main shrouds, guys had been stretched, just low enough

for the foreboom to swing clear; and from each of these guys at least fifty bunches of bananas were suspended.

It promised to be a messy passage, even if we did make it in the two or three days that would have been required if the south-east trades had been blowing fresh. But they weren't blowing fresh. After the first five hours the trade died away in a dozen or so gasping fans. The calm continued all that night and the next day—one of those glaring, glassy calms, when the very thought of opening one's eyes to look at it is sufficient to cause a headache.

The second day a man died—an Easter Islander, one of the best divers that season in the lagoon. Smallpox—that is what it was; though how smallpox could come on board, when there had been no known cases ashore when we left Rangiroa, is beyond me. There it was, though—smallpox, a man dead, and three others down on their backs.

There was nothing to be done. We could not segregate the sick, nor could we care for them. We were packed like sardines. There was nothing to do but rot and die—that is, there was nothing to do after the night that followed the first death. On that night the mate, the supercargo, the Polish Jew, and four native divers sneaked away in the large whale-boat. They were never heard of again. In the morning the captain promptly scuttled the remaining boats, and there we were.

That day there were two deaths; the following day three; then it jumped to eight. It was curious to see how we took it. The natives, for instance, fell into a condition of dumb, stolid fear. The captain—Oudouse, his name was, a Frenchman—became very nervous and voluble. He actually got the twitches. He was a large, fleshy man, weighing at least two hundred pounds, and he quickly became a faithful representation of a quivering jelly mountain of fat.

The German, the two Americans, and myself bought up all the Scotch whisky and proceeded to stay drunk. The theory was beautiful—namely, if we kept ourselves soaked in alcohol, every smallpox germ that came into contact with us would immediately be scorched to a cinder. And the theory worked, though I must confess that neither Captain Oudouse nor Ah Choon was attacked by the disease either. The Frenchman did not drink at all, while Ah Choon restricted himself to one drink daily.

It was a pretty time. The sun, going into northern declination, was straight overhead. There was no wind, except for frequent squalls, which blew fiercely for from five minutes to half an hour, and wound up by deluging us with rain. After each squall the awful sun would come out, drawing clouds of steam from the soaked decks.

The steam was not nice. It was the vapour of death, freighted with millions and millions of germs. We always took another drink when we saw it going up from the dead and dying, and usually we took two or three more drinks, mixing them exceptionally stiff. Also we made it a rule to take an additional several each time they hove the dead over to the sharks that swarmed about us.

We had a week of it, and then the whisky gave out. It is just as well, or I shouldn't be alive now. It took a sober man to pull through what followed, as you will agree when I mention the little fact that only two men did pull through. The other man was the heathen—at least, that was what I heard Captain Oudouse call him at the moment I first became aware of the heathen's existence. But to come back.

It was at the end of the week, with the whisky gone and the pearl buyers sober, that I happened to glance at the barometer that hung in the cabin companion-way. Its normal register in the Paumotas was 29·90, and it was quite customary to see it vacillate between 29·85 and 30·00, or even 30·05; but to see it as I saw it, down to 29·62, was sufficient to sober the most drunken pearl buyer that ever incinerated smallpox microbes in Scotch whisky.

I called Captain Oudouse's attention to it, only to be informed that he had watched it going down for several hours. There was little to do, but that little he did very well, considering the circumstances. He took off the light sails, shortened right down to storm canvas, spread life-lines, and waited for the wind. His mistake lay in what he did after the wind came. He hove to on the port tack, which was the right thing to do south of the Equator if—and there was the rub—*if* one were *not* in the direct path of the hurricane.

We were in the direct path. I could see that by the steady increase of the wind and the equally steady fall of the barometer. I wanted him to turn and run with the wind on the port quarters until the barometer ceased falling, and then to heave to. We argued till he was reduced to hysteria, but budge he would not. The worst of it was that I could not get the rest of the pearl buyers to back me up. Who was I, anyway, to know more about the sea and its ways than a properly qualified captain? was what was in their minds, I knew.

Of course the sea rose with the wind frightfully; and I shall never forget the first three seas the *Petite Jeanne* shipped. She had fallen off, as vessels do at times when hove to, and the first sea made a clean breach. The life-lines were only for the strong and well, and little good were they even for them when the women and children, the bananas and coconuts, the pigs and trade boxes, the sick and the dying, were swept along in a solid, screeching, groaning mass.

The second sea filled the *Petite Jeanne*'s decks flush with the rails; and as her stern sank down and her bow tossed skyward, all the miserable dunnage of life and luggage poured aft. It was a human torrent. They came head first, feet first, sideways, rolling over and over, twisting, squirming, writhing, and crumpling up. Now and again one caught a grip on a stanchion or a rope; but the weight of the bodies behind tore such grips loose.

One man I noticed fetched up, head on and square on, with the starboard bitt. His head cracked like an egg. I saw what was coming, sprang on top of the cabin, and from there into the mainsail itself. Ah Choon and one of the Americans tried to follow me, but I was one jump ahead of them. The American was swept away and over the stern like a piece of chaff. Ah Choon caught a spoke of the wheel and swung in behind it. But a strapping Rarotonga *wahine* (woman)—she must have weighed two hundred and fifty—brought up against him and got an arm around his neck. He clutched the Kanaka steersman with his other hand; and just at that moment the schooner flung down to starboard.

The rush of bodies and sea that was coming along the port runway between the captain and the rail turned abruptly and poured to starboard. Away they went—*wahine*, Ah Choon, and steersman; and I swear I saw Ah Choon grin at me with philosophic resignation as he cleared the rail and went under.

The third sea—the biggest of the three—did not do so much damage. By the time it arrived nearly everybody was in the rigging. On deck perhaps a dozen gasping, half-drowned, and half-stunned wretches were rolling about or attempting to crawl into safety. They went by the board, as did the wreckage of the two remaining boats. The other pearl buyers and myself, between seas, managed to get about fifteen women and children into the cabin and battened down. Little good it did the poor creatures in the end.

Wind? Out of all my experience I could not have believed it possible for the wind to blow as it did. There is no describing it. How can one describe a nightmare? It was the same way with that wind. It tore the clothes off our bodies. I say *tore them off*, and I mean it. I am not asking you to believe it. I am merely telling something that I saw and felt. There are times when I do not believe it myself. I went through it, and that is enough. One could not face that wind and live. It was a monstrous thing, and the most monstrous thing about it was that it increased and continued to increase.

Imagine countless millions and billions of tons of sand. Imagine this sand tearing along at ninety, a hundred, a hundred and twenty, or any other number of miles per hour. Imagine, further, this sand to be invisible, impalpable, yet to retain all the weight and density of sand. Do all this, and you may get a vague inkling of what that wind was like.

Perhaps sand is not the right comparison. Consider it mud, invisible, impalpable, but heavy as mud. Nay, it goes beyond

that. Consider every molecule of air to be a mud-bank in itself.
Then try to imagine the multitudinous impact of mudbanks.
No; it is beyond me. Language may be adequate to express the
ordinary conditions of life, but it cannot possibly express any
of the conditions of so enormous a blast of wind. It would have
been better had I stuck by my original intention of not attempting a description.

I will say this much: the sea, which had risen at first, was
beaten down by that wind. More, it seemed as if the whole
ocean had been sucked up in the maw of the hurricane, and
hurled on through that portion of space which previously had
been occupied by the air.

Of course our canvas had gone long before. But Captain
Oudouse had on the *Petite Jeanne* something I had never before
seen on a South Sea schooner—a sea anchor. It was a conical
canvas bag, the mouth of which was kept open by a huge
hoop of iron. The sea anchor was brindled something like a
kite, so that it bit into the water as a kite bites into the air, but
with a difference. The sea anchor remained just under the
surface of the ocean in a perpendicular position. A long line,
in turn, connected it with the schooner. As a result the
Petite Jeanne rode bow on to the wind and to what sea there
was.

The situation really would have been favourable had we
not been in the path of the storm. True, the wind itself tore
our canvas out of the gaskets, jerked out our topmasts, and
made a raffle of our running gear, but still we would have come
through nicely had we not been square in front of the advancing
storm-centre. That was what fixed us. I was in a state of
stunned, numbed, paralysed collapse from enduring the impact of the wind, and I think I was just about ready to give up
and die when the centre smote us. The blow we received was
an absolute lull. There was not a breath of air. The effect on
one was sickening.

Remember that for hours we had been at terrific muscular
tension, withstanding the awful pressure of that wind. And
then, suddenly, the pressure was removed. I know that I felt

D

as though I was about to expand, to fly apart in all directions. It seemed as if every atom composing my body was repelling every other atom and was on the verge of rushing off irresistibly into space. But that lasted only for a moment. Destruction was upon us.

In the absence of wind and pressure the sea rose. It jumped, it leaped, it soared straight towards the clouds. Remember, from every point of the compass that inconceivable wind was blowing in towards the centre of calm. The result was that the seas sprang up from every point of the compass. There was no wind to check them. They popped up like corks released from the bottom of a pail of water. There was no system to them, no stability. They were hollow, maniacal seas. They were eighty feet high at the least. They were not seas at all. They resembled no sea a man had ever seen.

They were splashes, monstrous splashes—that is all. Splashes that were eighty feet high. Eighty! They were more than eighty. They went over our mastheads. They were spouts, explosions. They were drunken. They fell anywhere, anyhow. They jostled one another; they collided. They rushed together and collapsed upon one another, or fell apart like a thousand waterfalls all at once. It was no ocean any man had ever dreamed of, that hurricane-centre. It was confusion thrice confounded. It was anarchy. It was a hell-pit of sea water gone mad.

The *Petite Jeanne*? I don't know. The heathen told me afterwards that he did not know. She was literally torn apart, ripped wide open, beaten into a pulp, smashed into kindling wood, annihilated. When I came to I was in the water, swimming automatically, though I was about two-thirds drowned. How I got there I had no recollection. I remembered seeing the *Petite Jeanne* fly to pieces at what must have been the instant that my own consciousness was buffeted out of me. But there I was, with nothing to do but make the best of it, and in that best there was little promise. The wind was blowing again, the sea was much smaller and more regular, and I knew that I had passed through the centre. Fortunately there were no sharks about. The hurricane had dissipated the ravenous horde that had surrounded the death ship and fed off the dead.

It was about midday when the *Petite Jeanne* went to pieces. and it must have been two hours afterwards when I picked up with one of her hatch covers. Thick rain was driving at the time; and it was the merest chance that flung me and the hatch cover together. A short length of line was trailing from the rope handle; and I knew that I was good for a day, at least, if the sharks did not return. Three hours later, possibly a little longer, sticking close to the cover, and with closed eyes concentrating my whole soul upon the task of breathing in enough air to keep me going and at the same time of avoiding breathing in enough water to drown me, it seemed that I heard voices. The rain had ceased, and wind and sea were easing marvellously. Not twenty feet away from me, on another hatch cover, were Captain Oudouse and the heathen. They were fighting over possession of the cover—at least, the Frenchman was.

'*Païen noir!*' I heard him scream, and at the same time I saw him kick the Kanaka.

Now Captain Oudouse had lost all his clothes except his shoes, and they were heavy brogans. It was a cruel blow, for it caught the heathen on the mouth and the point of the chin, half stunning him. I looked for him to retaliate, but he contented himself with swimming about forlornly a safe ten feet away. Whenever a fling of the sea threw him closer, the Frenchman, hanging on with his hands, kicked out at him with both feet. Also, at the moment of delivering each kick, he called the Kanaka a black heathen.

'For two centimes I'd come over there and drown you, you white beast!' I yelled.

The only reason I did not go was that I felt too tired. The very thought of the effort to swim over was nauseating. So I called to the Kanaka to come to me, and proceeded to share the hatch with him. Otoo, he told me his name was (pronounced ō-tō-ō); also he told me that he was a native of Borabora, the most westerly of the Society group. As I learned afterwards, he had got the hatch cover first, and, after some time, encountering Captain Oudouse, had offered to share it with him, and had been kicked off for his pains.

And that was how Otoo and I first came together. He was no fighter. He was all sweetness and gentleness, a love creature, though he stood nearly six feet tall and was muscled like a gladiator. He was no fighter, but he was also no coward. He had the heart of a lion; and in the years that followed I have seen him run risks that I would never dream of taking. What I mean is that while he was no fighter, and while he always avoided precipitating a row, he never ran away from trouble when it started. And it was "Ware shoal!" when once Otoo went into action. I shall never forget what he did to Bill King. It occurred in German Samoa. Bill King was hailed the champion heavyweight of the American Navy. He was a big brute of a man, a veritable gorilla, one of those hard-hitting, rough-housing chaps, and clever with his fists as well. He picked the quarrel, and he kicked Otoo twice and struck him once before Otoo felt it to be necessary to fight. I don't think it lasted four minutes, at the end of which time Bill King was the unhappy possessor of four broken ribs, a broken forearm, and a dislocated shoulder blade. Otoo knew nothing of scientific boxing. He was merely a manhandler; and Bill King was something like three months in recovering from the bit of manhandling he received that afternoon on Apia beach.

But I am running ahead of my yarn. We shared the hatch cover between us. We took turn and turn about, one lying flat on the cover and resting, while the other, submerged to the neck, merely held on with his hands. For two days and nights, spell and spell, on the cover and in the water, we drifted over the ocean. Towards the last I was delirious most of the time; and there were times, too, when I heard Otoo babbling and raving in his native tongue. Our continuous immersion prevented us from dying of thirst, though the sea water and the sunshine gave us the prettiest imaginable combination of salt-pickle and sunburn.

In the end Otoo saved my life; for I came to lying on the

beach twenty feet from the water, sheltered from the sun by a couple of coconut leaves. No one but Otoo could have dragged me there and struck up the leaves for shade. He was lying beside me. I went off again; and the next time I came round it was cool and starry night, and Otoo was pressing a drinking coconut to my lips.

We were the sole survivors of the *Petite Jeanne*. Captain Oudouse must have succumbed to exhaustion, for several days later his hatch cover drifted ashore without him. Otoo and I lived with the natives of the atoll for a week, when we were rescued by the French cruiser and taken to Tahiti. In the meantime, however, we had performed the ceremony of exchanging names. In the South Seas such a ceremony binds two men closer together than blood brothership. The initiative had been mine; and Otoo was rapturously delighted when I suggested it.

'It is well,' he said in Tahitian. 'For we have been mates together for two days on the lips of Death.'

'But Death stuttered,' I smiled.

'It was a brave deed you did, master,' he replied, 'and Death was not vile enough to speak.'

'Why do you "master" me?' I demanded with a show of hurt feelings. 'We have exchanged names. To you I am Otoo. To me you are Charley. And between you and me, for ever and for ever, you shall be Charley, and I shall be Otoo. It is the way of the custom. And when we die, if it does happen that we live again somewhere beyond the stars and the sky, still shall you be Charley to me, and I Otoo to you.'

'Yes, master,' he answered, his eyes luminous and soft with joy.

'There you go!' I cried indignantly.

'What does it matter what my lips utter?' he argued. 'They are only my lips. But I shall think Otoo always. Whenever I think of myself, I shall think of you. Whenever men call me by name, I shall think of you. And beyond the sky and beyond the stars, always and for ever, you shall be Otoo to me. Is it well, master?'

I hid my smile and answered that it was well.

We parted at Papeete. I remained ashore to recuperate; and he went on in a cutter to his own island, Borabora. Six weeks later he was back. I was surprised, for he had told me of his wife, and said that he was returning to her, and would give over sailing on far voyages.

'Where do you go, master?' he asked after our first greetings.

I shrugged my shoulders. It was a hard question.

'All the world,' was my answer, 'all the world, all the sea, and all the islands that are in the sea.'

'I will go with you,' he said simply. 'My wife is dead.'

I never had a brother; but from what I have seen of other men's brothers, I doubt if any man ever had a brother that was to him what Otoo was to me. He was brother and father and mother as well. And this I know: I lived a straighter and better man because of Otoo. I cared little for other men, but I had to live straight in Otoo's eyes. Because of him I dared not tarnish myself. He made me his ideal, compounding me, I fear, chiefly out of his own love and worship; and there were times when I stood close to the steep pitch of hell, and would have taken the plunge had not the thought of Otoo restrained me. His pride in me entered into me, until it became one of the major rules in my personal code to do nothing that would diminish that pride of his.

Naturally I did not learn right away what his feelings were towards me. He never criticized, never censured; and slowly the exalted place I held in his eyes dawned upon me, and slowly I grew to comprehend the hurt I could inflict upon him by being anything less than my best.

For seventeen years we were together; for seventeen years he was at my shoulder, watching while I slept, nursing me through fever and wounds—aye, and receiving wounds in fighting for me. He signed on the same ships with me; and together we ranged the Pacific from Hawaii to Sydney Head, and from Torres Straits to the Galapagos. We blackbirded from the New Hebrides and the Line Islands over to the westward clear through the Louisiades, New Britain, New

Ireland, and New Hanover. We were wrecked three times—in the Gilberts, in the Santa Cruz group, and in the Fijis. And we traded and salved wherever a dollar promised in the way of pearl and pearly shell, copra, bêche-de-mer, hawkbill turtle shell, and stranded wrecks.

It began in Papeete, immediately after his announcement that he was going with me all over the sea, and the islands in the midst thereof. There was a club in those days in Papeete, where the pearlers, traders, captains, and riffraff of South Sea adventurers forgathered. The play ran high, and the drink ran high; and I am very much afraid that I kept later hours than were becoming or proper. No matter what the hour was when I left the club, there was Otoo waiting to see me safely home.

At first I smiled; next I chided him. Then I told him flatly that I stood in need of no wet-nursing. After that I did not see him when I came out of the club. Quite by accident, a week or so later, I discovered that he still saw me home, lurking across the street among the shadows of the mango trees. What could I do? I know what I did do.

Insensibly I began to keep better hours. On wet and stormy nights, in the thick of the folly and the fun, the thought would persist in coming to me of Otoo keeping his dreary vigil under the dripping mangoes. Truly, he made a better man of me. Yet he was not strait-laced. And he knew nothing of common Christian morality. All the people on Borabora were Christians; but he was a heathen, the only unbeliever on the island, a gross materialist, who believed that when he died he was dead. He believed merely in fair play and square dealing. Petty meanness, in his code, was almost as serious as wanton homicide; and I do believe that he respected a murderer more than a man given to small practices.

Concerning me, personally, he objected to my doing anything that was hurtful to me. Gambling was all right. He was an ardent gambler himself. But late hours, he explained, were bad for one's health. He had seen men who did not take care of themselves die of fever. He was no teetotaller, and welcomed a stiff nip at any time when it was wet work in the boats. On the other hand, he believed in liquor in moderation. He had seen many men killed or disgraced by squareface or Scotch.

Otoo had my welfare always at heart. He thought ahead for me, weighed my plans, and took a greater interest in them than I did myself. At first, when I was unaware of this interest of his in my affairs, he had to divine my intentions, as, for instance, at Papeete, when I contemplated going partners with a knavish fellow-countryman on a guana venture. I did not know he was a knave. Nor did any white man in Papeete. Neither did Otoo know, but he saw how thick we were getting, and found out for me, and without my asking him. Native sailors from the ends of the seas knock about on the beach in Tahiti; and Otoo, suspicious merely, went among them till he had gathered sufficient data to justify his suspicions. Oh, it was a nice history, that of Randolph Waters. I couldn't believe it when Otoo first narrated it; but when I sheeted it home to Waters he gave in without a murmur and got away on the first steamer to Auckland.

At first, I am free to confess, I couldn't help resenting Otoo's poking his nose into my business. But I knew that he was wholly unselfish; and soon I had to acknowledge his wisdom and discretion. He had his eyes open always to my main chance, and he was both keen-sighted and far-sighted. In time he became my counsellor, until he knew more of my business than I did myself. He really had my interest at heart more than I did. Mine was the magnificent carelessness of youth, for I preferred romance to dollars, and adventure to a comfortable billet with all night in. So it was well that I had someone to look out for me. I know that if it had not been for Otoo I should not be here today.

Of numerous instances, let me give one. I had had some experience in blackbirding before I went pearling in the Paumotas. Otoo and I were on the beach in Samoa—we really were on the beach and hard aground—when my chance came to go as recruiter on a blackbird brig. Otoo signed on before the mast; and for the next half-dozen years, in as many ships, we knocked about the wildest portions of Melanesia. Otoo saw to it that he always pulled stroke oar in my boat. Our custom in recruiting labour was to land the recruiter on the beach. The covering boat always lay on its oars several hundred feet offshore, while the recruiter's boat, also lying on its oars, kept afloat on the edge of the beach. When I landed with my trade goods, leaving my steering sweep apeak, Otoo left his stroke position and came into the stern sheets, where a Winchester lay ready to hand under a flap of canvas. The boat's crew was also armed, the Sniders concealed under canvas flaps that ran the length of the gunwales. While I was busy arguing and persuading the woolly-headed cannibals to come and labour on the Queensland plantations, Otoo kept watch. And often his low voice warned me of suspicious actions and impending treachery. Sometimes it was the quick shot from his rifle that was the first warning I received. And in my rush to the boat his hand was always there to jerk me flying aboard. Once, I remember, on *Santa Anna*, the boat grounded just as the trouble began. The covering boat was dashing to our assistance, but the several score of savages would have wiped us out before it arrived. Otoo took a flying leap ashore, dug both hands in the trade goods, and scattered tobacco, beads, tomahawks, knives, and calicoes in all directions.

This was too much for the woolly-heads. While they scrambled for the treasures, the boat was shoved clear, and we were aboard and forty feet away. And I got thirty recruits off that very beach in the next four hours.

The particular instance I have in mind was on Malaita, the most savage island in the easterly Solomons. The natives had been remarkably friendly; and how were we to know that the whole village had been taking up a collection for over two years with which to buy a white man's head? The beggars are all head-hunters, and they especially esteem a white man's head. The fellow who captured the head would receive the whole collection. As I say, they appeared very friendly; and on this day I was fully a hundred yards down the beach from the boat. Otoo had cautioned me; and, as usual when I did not heed him, I came to grief.

The first I knew, a cloud of spears sailed out of the mangrove swamp at me. At least a dozen were sticking into me. I started to run, but tripped over one that was fast in my calf, and went down. The woolly-heads made a run for me, each with a long-handled, fantail tomahawk with which to hack off my head. They were so eager for the prize that they got in one another's way. In the confusion I avoided several hacks by throwing myself right and left on the sand.

Then Otoo arrived—Otoo the manhandler. In some way he had got hold of a heavy war club, and at close quarters it was a far more efficient weapon than a rifle. He was right in the thick of them, so that they could not spear him, while their tomahawks seemed worse than useless. He was fighting for me, and he was in a true berserker rage. The way he handled that club was amazing. Their skulls squashed like over-ripe oranges. It was not until he had driven them back, picked me up in his arms, and started to run that he received his first wounds. He arrived in the boat with four spear thrusts, got his Winchester, and with it got a man with every shot. Then we pulled aboard the schooner and doctored up.

Seventeen years we were together. He made me. I should today be a supercargo, a recruiter, or a memory, if it had not been for him.

'You spend your money, and you go out and get more,' he said one day. 'It is easy to get money now. But when you get old, your money will be spent, and you will not be able to go out and get more. I know, master. I have studied the way of white men. On the beaches are many old men who were young once, and who could get money just like you. Now they are old, and they have nothing, and they wait about for the young men like you to come ashore and buy drinks for them.

'The black boy is a slave on the plantations. He gets twenty dollars a year. He works hard. The overseer does not work hard. He rides a horse and watches the black boy work. He gets twelve hundred dollars a year. I am a sailor on the schooner. I get fifteen dollars a month. That is because I am a good sailor. I work hard. The captain has a double awning and drinks beer out of long bottles. I have never seen him haul a rope or pull an oar. He gets one hundred and fifty dollars a month. I am a sailor. He is a navigator. Master, I think it would be very good for you to know navigation.'

Otoo spurred me on to it. He sailed with me as second mate on my first schooner, and he was far prouder of my command than I was myself. Later on it was:

'The captain is well paid, master; but the ship is in his keeping, and he is never free from the burden. It is the owner who is better paid—and the owner who sits ashore with many servants and turns his money over.'

'True, but a schooner costs five thousand dollars—an old schooner at that,' I objected. 'I should be an old man before I saved five thousand dollars.'

'There be short ways for white men to make money,' he went on, pointing ashore at the coconut-fringed beach.

We were in the Solomons at the time, picking up a cargo of ivory nuts along the east coast of Guadalcanal.

'Between this river mouth and the next it is two miles,' he said. 'The flat land runs far back. It is worth nothing now. Next year—who knows?—or the year after, men will pay much money for that land. The anchorage is good. Big steamers can lie close up. You can buy the land four miles deep from the old chief for ten thousand sticks of tobacco, ten bottles of squareface, and a Snider, which will cost you, maybe, one hundred dollars. Then you place the deed with the commissioner; and the next year, or the year after, you sell and become the owner of a ship.'

I followed his lead, and his words came true, though in three years instead of two. Next came the grasslands deal on Guadalcanal—twenty thousand acres, on a governmental nine hundred and ninety-nine years' lease at a nominal sum. I owned the lease for precisely ninety days, when I sold it to a company for half a fortune. Always it was Otoo who looked ahead and saw the opportunity. He was responsible for the salving of the *Doncaster*—bought in at auction for a hundred pounds, and clearing three thousand after every expense was paid. He led me into the Savaii plantation and the cocoa venture on Upolu.

We did not go seafaring so much as in the old days. I was too well off. I married, and my standard of living rose; but Otoo remained the same old-time Otoo, moving about the house or trailing through the office, his wooden pipe in his mouth, a shilling undershirt on his back, and a four-shilling lava-lava about his loins. I could not get him to spend money. There was no way of repaying him except with love, and God knows he got that in full measure from all of us. The children worshipped him and if he had been spoilable, my wife would surely have been his undoing.

The children! He really was the one who showed them the way of their feet in the world practical. He began by teaching them to walk. He sat up with them when they were sick. One by one, when they were scarcely toddlers, he took them down to the lagoon and made them into amphibians. He taught them more than I ever knew of the habits of fish and the ways of catching them. In the bush it was the same thing. At seven Tom knew more woodcraft than I ever dreamed existed. At six Mary went over the Sliding Rock without a quiver, and I had seen strong men balk at that feat. And when Frank had just turned six he could bring up shillings from the bottom in three fathoms.

'My people in Borabora do not like heathen—they are all Christians; and I do not like Borabora Christians,' he said one day, when I, with the idea of getting him to spend some of the money that was rightfully his, had been trying to persuade him to make a visit to his own island in one of our schooners—a special voyage which I had hoped to make a record breaker in the matter of prodigal expense.

I say one of *our* schooners, though legally at the time they belonged to me. I struggled long with him to enter into partnership.

'We have been partners from the day the *Petite Jeanne* went down,' he said at last. 'But if your heart so wishes, then shall we become partners by the law. I have no work to do, yet are my expenses large. I drink and eat and smoke in plenty—it costs much, I know. I do not pay for the playing of billiards, for I play on your table; but still the money goes. Fishing on the reef is only a rich man's pleasure. It is shocking, the cost of hooks and cotton line. Yes; it is necessary that we be partners by law, I need the money. I shall get it from the head clerk in the office.'

So the papers were made out and recorded. A year later I was compelled to complain.

'Charley,' said I, 'you are a wicked old fraud, a miserly skinflint, a miserable land crab. Behold, your share for the year in all our partnerships has been thousands of dollars. The head clerk has given me this paper. It says that in the year you have drawn just eighty-seven dollars and twenty cents.'

'Is there any owing me?' he asked anxiously.

'I tell you thousands and thousands,' I answered.

His face brightened, as with an immense relief.

'It is well,' he said. 'See that the head clerk keeps good account of it. When I want it, I shall want it, and there must not be a cent missing.'

'If there is,' he added fiercely, after a pause, 'it must come out of the clerk's wages.'

And all the time, as I afterwards learned, his will, drawn up by Carruthers, and making me sole beneficiary, lay in the American consul's safe.

But the end came, as the end must come to all human associations. It occurred in the Solomons, where our wildest work had been done in the wild young days, and where we were once more—principally on a holiday, incidentally to look after our holdings on Florida Island and to look over the pearling possibilities of the Mboli Pass. We were lying at Savu, having run in to trade for curios.

Now Savu is alive with sharks. The custom of the woolly-heads of burying their dead in the sea did not tend to discourage the sharks from making the adjacent waters a hangout. It was my luck to be coming aboard in a tiny, overloaded, native canoe when the thing capsized. There were four woolly-heads and myself in it, or, rather hanging to it. The schooner was a hundred yards away. I was just hailing for a boat when one of the woolly-heads began to scream. Holding on to the end of the canoe, both he and that portion of the canoe were dragged under several times. Then he loosed his clutch and disappeared. A shark had got him.

The three remaining woolly-heads tried to climb out of the water upon the bottom of the canoe. I yelled and cursed and struck at the nearest with my fist, but it was no use. They were in a blind funk. The canoe could barely have supported one of them. Under the three it upended and rolled sideways, throwing them back into the water.

I abandoned the canoe and started to swim towards the schooner, expecting to be picked up by the boat before I got there. One of the woolly-heads elected to come with me, and we swam along silently, side by side, now and again putting our faces into the water and peering about for sharks. The screams of the man who stayed by the canoe informed us that he was taken. I was peering into the water when I saw a big shark pass directly beneath me. He was fully sixteen feet in length. I saw the whole thing. He got the woolly-head by the middle, and away he went, the poor devil, head, shoulders, and arms out of water all the time, screeching in a heart-rending way. He was carried along in this fashion for several hundred feet, when he was dragged beneath the surface.

I swam doggedly on, hoping that that was the last unattached shark. But there was another. Whether it was one that had attacked the natives earlier, or whether it was one that had made a good meal elsewhere, I do not know. At any rate, he was not in such haste as the others. I could not swim so rapidly now, for a large part of my effort was devoted to keeping track of him. I was watching him when he made his first attack. By good luck I got both hands on his nose, and though his momentum nearly shoved me under, I managed to keep him off. He veered clear and began circling about again. A second time I escaped him by the same manœuvre.

The third rush was a miss on both sides. He sheered at the moment my hands should have landed on his nose, but his sandpaper hide (I had on a sleeveless undershirt) scraped the skin off one arm from elbow to shoulder.

By this time I was played out, and gave up hope. The schooner was still two hundred feet away. My face was in the water, and I was watching him manœuvre for another attempt, when I saw a brown body pass between us. It was Otoo.

'Swim for the schooner, master!' he said. And he spoke gaily, as though the affair was a mere lark. 'I know sharks. The shark is my brother.'

I obeyed, swimming slowly on, while Otoo swam about me, keeping always between me and the shark, foiling his rushes and encouraging me.

'The davit tackle carried away, and they are rigging the falls,' he explained a minute or so later, and then went under to head off another attack.

By the time the schooner was thirty feet away I was about done for. I could scarcely move. They were heaving lines at us from on board, but they continually fell short. The shark, finding that it was receiving no hurt, had become bolder. Several times it nearly got me, but each time Otoo was there just the moment before it was too late. Of course Otoo could have saved himself any time. But he stuck by me.

'Good-bye, Charley! I'm finished!' I just managed to gasp.

I knew that the end had come, and that the next moment I should throw up my hands and go down.

But Otoo laughed in my face, saying:

'I will show you a new trick. I will make that shark feel sick!'

He dropped in behind me, where the shark was preparing to come at me.

'A little more to the left!' he next called out. 'There is a line there on the water. To the left, master—to the left!'

I changed my course and struck out blindly. I was by that time barely conscious. As my hands closed on the line I heard an exclamation from on board. I turned and looked. There was no sign of Otoo. The next instant he broke surface. Both hands were off at the wrist, the stumps spouting blood.

'Otoo!' he called softly. And I could see in his gaze the love that thrilled in his voice.

Then, and then only, at the very last of all our years, he called me by that name.

'Good-bye, Otoo!' he called.

Then he was dragged under, and I was hauled aboard, where I fainted in the captain's arms.

And so passed Otoo, who saved me and made me a man and who saved me in the end. We met in the maw of a hurricane and parted in the maw of a shark, with seventeen intervening years of comradeship, the like of which I dare to assert has never befallen two men, the one brown and the other white. If Jehovah be from His high place watching every sparrow fall, not least in His kingdom shall be Otoo, the one heathen of Borabora.

To Build a Fire

DAY had broken cold and grey, exceedingly cold and grey, when the man turned aside from the main Yukon trail and climbed the high earth-bank, where a dim and little-travelled trail led eastward through the fat spruce timberland. It was a steep bank, and he paused for breath at the top, excusing the act to himself by looking at his watch. It was nine o'clock. There was no sun nor hint of sun, though there was not a cloud in the sky. It was a clear day, and yet there seemed an intangible pall over the face of things, a subtle gloom that made the day dark, and that was due to the absence of sun. This fact did not worry the man. He was used to the lack of sun. It had been days since he had seen the sun, and he knew that a few more days must pass before that cheerful orb, due south, would just peep above the skyline and dip immediately from view.

The man flung a look back along the way he had come. The Yukon lay a mile wide and hidden under three feet of ice. On top of this ice were as many feet of snow. It was all pure white, rolling in gentle undulations where the ice jams of the freeze-up had formed. North and south, as far as his eye could see, it was unbroken white, save for a dark hairline that curved and twisted from around the spruce-covered island to the south, and that curved and twisted away into the north, where it disappeared behind another spruce-covered island. This dark hairline was the trail—the main trail—that led south five hundred miles to the Chilcoot Pass, Dyea, and salt water; and that led north seventy miles to Dawson, and still on to the north a thousand miles to Nulato, and finally to St. Michael, on Bering Sea, a thousand miles and half a thousand more.

But all this—the mysterious, far-reaching hairline trail, the absence of sun from the sky, the tremendous cold, and the strangeness and weirdness of it all—made no impression on the man. It was not because he was long used to it. He was a newcomer in the land, a *chechaquo*, and this was his first winter. The trouble with him was that he was without imagination. He was quick and alert in the things of life, but only in the things, and not in the significances. Fifty degrees below zero meant eighty-odd degrees of frost. Such fact impressed him as being cold and uncomfortable, and that was all. It did not lead him to meditate upon his frailty as a creature of temperature, and upon man's frailty in general, able only to live within certain narrow limits of heat and cold; and from there on it did not lead him to the conjectural field of immortality and man's place in the universe. Fifty degrees below zero stood for a bite of frost that hurt and that must be guarded against by the use of mittens, ear flaps, warm moccasins, and thick socks. Fifty degrees below zero. That there should be anything more to it than that was a thought that never entered his head.

As he turned to go on, he spat speculatively. There was a sharp explosive crackle that startled him. He spat again. And again, in the air, before it could fall to the snow, the spittle crackled. He knew that at fifty below spittle crackled on the snow, but this spittle had crackled in the air. Undoubtedly it was colder than fifty below—how much colder he did not know. But the temperature did not matter. He was bound for the old claim on the left fork of Henderson Creek, where the boys were already. They had come over across the divide from the Indian Creek country, while he had come the roundabout way to take a look at the possibilities of getting out logs in the spring from the islands in the Yukon. He would be in to camp by six o'clock; a bit after dark, it was true, but the boys would be there, a fire would be going, and a hot supper would be ready. As for lunch, he pressed his hand against the protruding bundle under his jacket. It was also under his shirt, wrapped up in a handkerchief and lying against the naked skin. It was the only way to keep the biscuits from freezing. He smiled agreeably to himself as he thought of those biscuits, each cut open and sopped in bacon grease, and each enclosing a generous slice of fried bacon.

He plunged in among the big spruce trees. The trail was

faint. A foot of snow had fallen since the last sled had passed over, and he was glad he was without a sled, travelling light. In fact, he carried nothing but the lunch wrapped in the handkerchief. He was surprised, however, at the cold. It certainly was cold, he concluded, as he rubbed his numb nose and cheek-bones with his mittened hand. He was a warm-whiskered man, but the hair on his face did not protect the high cheek-bones and the eager nose that thrust itself aggressively into the frosty air.

At the man's heels trotted a dog, a big native husky, the proper wolf-dog, grey-coated and without any visible or temperamental difference from its brother, the wild wolf. The animal was depressed by the tremendous cold. It knew that it was no time for travelling. Its instinct told it a truer tale than was told to the man by the man's judgement. In reality, it was not merely colder than fifty below zero; it was colder than sixty below, than seventy below. It was seventy-five below zero. Since the freezing point is thirty-two above zero, it meant that one hundred and seven degrees of frost obtained. The dog did not know anything about thermometers. Possibly in its brain there was no sharp consciousness of a condition of very cold such as was in the man's brain. But the brute had its instinct. It experienced a vague but menacing apprehension that subdued it and made it slink along at the man's heels, and that made it question eagerly every unwonted movement of the man as if expecting him to go into camp or to seek shelter somewhere and build a fire. The dog had learned fire, and it wanted fire, or else to burrow under the snow and cuddle its warmth away from the air.

The frozen moisture of its breathing had settled on its fur in a fine powder of frost, and especially were its jowls, muzzle, and eyelashes whitened by its crystal breath. The man's red beard and moustache were likewise frosted, but more solidly, the deposit taking the form of ice and increasing with every warm, moist breath he exhaled. Also, the man was chewing tobacco, and the muzzle of ice held his lips so rigidly that he was unable to clear his chin when he expelled the juice. The result was a crystal beard of the colour and solidity of amber was increasing its length on his chin. If he fell down it would shatter itself, like glass, into brittle fragments. But he did not mind the appendage. It was the penalty all tobacco chewers paid in that country, and he had been out before in two cold snaps. They had not been so cold as this, he knew, but by the spirit thermometer at Sixty Mile he knew they had been registered at fifty below and at fifty-five.

He held on through the level stretch of woods for several miles, crossed a wide flat of nigger heads, and dropped down a bank to the frozen bed of a small stream. This was Henderson Creek, and he knew he was ten miles from the forks. He looked at his watch. It was ten o'clock. He was making four miles an hour, and he calculated that he would arrive at the forks at half-past twelve. He decided to celebrate that event by eating his lunch there.

The dog dropped in again at his heels, with a tail drooping discouragement, as the man swung along the creek bed. The furrow of the old sled trail was plainly visible, but a dozen inches of snow covered up the marks of the last runners. In a month no man had come up or down that silent creek. The man held steadily on. He was not much given to thinking, and just then particularly he had nothing to think about save that he would eat lunch at the forks and that at six o'clock he would be in camp with the boys. There was nobody to talk to; and, had there been, speech would have been impossible because of the ice muzzle on his mouth. So he continued monotonously to chew tobacco and to increase the length of his amber beard.

Once in a while the thought reiterated itself that it was very cold and that he had never experienced such cold. As he walked along he rubbed his cheek-bones and nose with the back of his mittened hand. He did this automatically, now and again changing hands. But, rub as he would, the instant he stopped his cheek-bones went numb, and the following instant the end of his nose went numb. He was sure to frost his cheeks; he knew that, and experienced a pang of regret that he had not devised a nose strap of the sort Bud wore in cold snaps. Such a strap passed across the cheeks, as well, and saved them. But it didn't matter much, after all. What were frosted cheeks? A bit painful, that was all; they were never serious.

Empty as the man's mind was of thoughts, he was keenly observant, and he noticed the changes in the creeks, the curves and bends and timber jams, and always he sharply noted where he placed his feet. Once, coming round a bend, he shied abruptly, like a startled horse, curved away from the place where he had been walking, and retreated several paces back along the trail. The creek he knew was frozen clear to the bottom—no creek could contain water in that arctic winter— but he knew also that there were springs that bubbled out from the hillsides and ran along under the snow and on top of the ice of the creek. He knew that the coldest snaps never froze these springs, and he knew likewise their danger. They were traps. They hid pools of water under the snow that might be three inches deep, or three feet. Sometimes a skin of ice half an inch thick covered them, and in turn was covered by the snow. Sometimes there were alternate layers of water and ice skin, so that when one broke through he kept on breaking through for a while, sometimes wetting himself to the waist.

That was why he had shied in such a panic. He had felt the give under his feet and heard the crackle of a snow-hidden ice skin. And to get his feet wet in such a temperature meant trouble and danger. At the very least it meant delay, for he would be forced to stop and build a fire, and under its pro- tection to bare his feet while he dried his socks and moccasins. He stood and studied the creek bed and its banks, and decided that the flow of water came from the right. He reflected awhile, rubbing his nose and cheeks, then skirted to the left, stepping gingerly and testing the footing for each step. Once clear of the danger, he took a fresh chew of tobacco and swung along at his four-mile gait.

In the course of the next two hours he came upon several similar traps. Usually the snow above the hidden pools had a sunken, candied appearance that advertised the danger. Once again, however, he had a close call; and once, suspecting danger, he compelled the dog to go on in front. The dog did not want to go. It hung back until the man shoved it forward, and then it went quickly across the white, unbroken surface. Suddenly it broke through, floundered to one side, and got away to firmer footing. It had wet its forefeet and legs, and almost immediately the water that clung to it turned to ice. It made quick efforts to lick the ice off its legs, then dropped down in the snow and began to bite out the ice that had formed between the toes. This was a matter of instinct. To permit the ice to remain would mean sore feet. It did not know this. It merely obeyed the mysterious prompting that arose from the deep crypts of its being. But the man knew, having achieved a judgement on the subject, and he removed the mitten from his right hand and helped to tear out the ice particles. He did not expose his fingers more than a minute, and was astonished at the swift numbness that smote them. It certainly was cold. He pulled on the mitten hastily, and beat the hand savagely across his chest.

At twelve o'clock the day was at its brightest. Yet the sun was too far south on its winter journey to clear the horizon. The bulge of the earth intervened between it and Henderson Creek, where the man walked under a clear sky at noon and cast no shadow. At half-past twelve, to the minute, he arrived at the forks of the creek. He was pleased at the speed he had made. If he kept it up, he would certainly be with the boys by six. He unbuttoned his jacket and shirt and drew forth his lunch. The action consumed no more than a quarter of a minute, yet in that brief moment the numbness laid hold of the exposed fingers. He did not put the mitten on, but, instead, struck the fingers a dozen sharp smashes against his leg. Then he sat down on a snow-covered log to eat. The sting that followed upon the striking of his fingers against his leg ceased so quickly that he was startled. He had had no chance to take a bite of biscuit. He struck the fingers repeatedly and returned them to the mitten, baring the other hand for the purpose of eating. He tried to take a mouthful, but the ice muzzle prevented. He had forgotten to build a fire and thaw out. He chuckled at his foolishness, and as he chuckled he noted the numbness creeping into the exposed fingers. Also, he noted that the stinging which had first come to his toes when he sat down was already passing away. He wondered whether the toes were warm or numb. He moved them inside the moccasins and decided that they were numb.

He pulled the mitten on hurriedly and stood up. He was a bit frightened. He stamped up and down until the stinging returned into the feet. It certainly was cold, was his thought. That man from Sulphur Creek had spoken the truth when telling how cold it sometimes got in the country. And he had laughed at him at the time! That showed one must not be too sure of things. There was no mistake about it, it *was* cold. He strode up and down, stamping his feet and threshing his arms, until reassured by the returning warmth. Then he got out matches and proceeded to make a fire. From the under-growth, where high water of the previous spring had lodged a supply of seasoned twigs, he got his firewood. Working carefully from a small beginning, he soon had a roaring fire, over which he thawed the ice from his face and in the protection of which he ate his biscuits. For the moment the cold of space was outwitted. The dog took satisfaction in the fire, stretching out close enough for warmth and far enough away to escape being singed.

When the man had finished, he filled his pipe and took his comfortable time over a smoke. Then he pulled on his mittens, settled the ear-flaps of his cap firmly about his ears, and took the creek trail up the left fork. The dog was disappointed and yearned back towards the fire. This man did not know cold. Possibly all the generations of his ancestry had been ignorant of cold, of real cold, of cold one hundred and seven degrees below freezing point. But the dog knew; all its ancestry knew, and it had inherited the knowledge. And it knew that it was not good to walk abroad in such fearful cold. It was the time to lie snug in a hole in the snow and wait for a curtain of cloud to be drawn across the face of outer space whence this cold came. On the other hand, there was no keen intimacy between the dog and the man. The one was the toil slave of the other, and the only caresses it had ever received were the caresses of the whip lash and of harsh and menacing throat sounds that threatened the whip lash. So the dog made no effort to communicate its apprehension to the man. It was not concerned in the welfare of the man; it was for its own sake that it yearned back towards the fire. But the man whistled, and spoke to it with the sound of whip lashes, and the dog swung in at the man's heels and followed after.

The man took a chew of tobacco and proceeded to start a new amber beard. Also, his moist breath quickly powdered with white his moustache, eyebrows, and lashes. There did not seem to be so many springs on the left fork of the Henderson, and for half an hour the man saw no signs of any. And then it happened. At a place where there were no signs, where the soft, unbroken snow seemed to advertise solidity beneath, the man broke through. It was not deep. He wet himself half-way to the knees before he floundered out to the firm crust.

He was angry, and cursed his luck aloud. He had hoped to get into camp with the boys at six o'clock, and this would delay him an hour, for he would have to build a fire and dry out his footgear. This was imperative at that low temperature —he knew that much; and he turned aside to the bank, which he climbed. On top, tangled in the underbrush about the trunks of several small spruce trees, was a high-water deposit of dry firewood—sticks and twigs, principally, but also larger portions of seasoned branches and fine, dry, last year's grasses. He threw down several large pieces on top of the snow. This served for a foundation and prevented the young flame from drowning itself in the snow it otherwise would melt. The flame he got by touching a match to a small shred of birch bark that he took from his pocket. This burned even more readily than paper. Placing it on the foundation, he fed the young flame with wisps of dry grass and with the tiniest dry twigs.

He worked slowly and carefully, keenly aware of his danger. Gradually, as the flame grew stronger, he increased the size of the twigs with which he fed it. He squatted in the snow pulling the twigs out from their entanglement in the brush and feeding directly to the flame. He knew there must be no failure. When it is seventy-five below zero, a man must not fail in his first attempt to build a fire—that is, if his feet are wet. If his feet are dry, and he fails, he can run along the trail for half a mile and restore his circulation. But the circulation of wet and freezing feet cannot be restored by running when it is seventy-five below. No matter how fast he runs, the wet feet will freeze the harder.

All this the man knew. The old-timer on Sulphur Creek had told him about it the previous fall, and now he was appreciating the advice. Already all sensation had gone out of his feet. To build the fire he had been forced to remove his mittens, and the fingers had quickly gone numb. His pace of four miles an hour had kept his heart pumping blood to the surface of his body and to all the extremities. But the instant he stopped, the action of the pump eased down. The cold of space smote the unprotected tip of the planet, and he, being on that unprotected tip, received the full force of the blow. The blood of his body recoiled before it. The blood was alive, like the dog, and like the dog it wanted to hide away and cover itself up from the fearful cold. So long as he walked four miles an hour, he pumped that blood, willy-nilly, to the surface; but now it ebbed away and sank down into the recesses of his body. The extremities were the first to feel its absence. His wet feet froze the faster, and his exposed fingers numbed the faster, though they had not yet begun to freeze. Nose and cheeks were already freezing, while the skin of all his body chilled as it lost its blood.

But he was safe. Toes and nose and cheeks would be only touched by the frost, for the fire was beginning to burn with strength. He was feeding it with twigs the size of his finger. In another minute he would be able to feed it with branches the size of his wrist, and then he could remove his wet footgear, and, while it dried, he could keep his naked feet warm by the fire, rubbing them at first, of course, with snow. The fire was a success. He was safe. He remembered the advice of the old-timer on Sulphur Creek, and smiled. The old-timer had been very serious in laying down the law that no man must travel alone in the Klondike after fifty below. Well, here he was; he had had the accident; he was alone; and he had saved himself. Those old-timers were rather womanish, some of them, he thought. All a man had to do was to keep his head, and he was all right. Any man who was a man could travel alone. But it was surprising, the rapidity with which his cheeks and nose were freezing. And he had not thought his fingers could go lifeless in so short a time. Lifeless they were, for he could scarcely make them move together to grip a twig, and they seemed remote from his body and from him. When he touched a twig, he had to look and see whether or not he had hold of it. The wires were pretty well down between him and his finger ends.

All of which counted for little. There was the fire, snapping and crackling and promising life with every dancing flame. He started to untie his moccasins. They were coated with ice; the thick German socks were like sheaths of iron half-way to the knees; and the moccasin strings were like rods of steel all twisted and knotted as by some conflagration. For a moment he tugged with his numb fingers, then, realizing the folly of it, he drew his sheath knife.

But before he could cut the strings, it happened. It was his own fault or, rather, his mistake. He should not have built the fire under the spruce tree. He should have built it in the open. But it had been easier to pull the twigs from the brush and drop them directly on the fire. Now the trees under which he had done this carried a weight of snow on its boughs. No wind had blown for weeks, and each bough was fully freighted. Each time he had pulled a twig he had communicated a slight agitation to the tree—an imperceptible agitation, so far as he was concerned, but an agitation sufficient to bring about the disaster. High up in the tree one bough capsized its load of snow. This fell on the boughs beneath, capsizing them. This process continued, spreading out and involving the whole tree.

It grew like an avalanche, and it descended without warning upon the man and the fire, and the fire was blotted out! Where it had burned was a mantle of fresh and disordered snow.

The man was shocked. It was as though he had just heard his own sentence of death. For a moment he sat and stared at the spot where the fire had been. Then he grew very calm. Perhaps the old-timer on Sulphur Creek was right. If he had only had a trail mate he would have been in no danger now. The trail mate could have built the fire. Well, it was up to him to build the fire over again, and this second time there must be no failure. Even if he succeeded, he would most likely lose some toes. His feet must be badly frozen by now, and there would be some time before the second fire was ready.

Such were his thoughts, but he did not sit and think them. He was busy all the time they were passing through his mind. He made a new foundation for a fire, this time in the open, where no treacherous tree could blot it out. Next he gathered dry grasses and tiny twigs from the high-water flotsam. He could not bring his fingers together to pull them out, but he was able to gather them by the handful. In this way he got many rotten twigs and bits of green moss that were undesirable, but it was the best he could do. He worked methodically, even collecting an armful of the larger branches to be used later when the fire gathered strength. And all the while the dog sat and watched him, a certain yearning wistfulness in its eyes, for it looked upon him as the fire provider, and the fire was slow in coming.

When all was ready, the man reached in his pocket for a second piece of birch bark. He knew the bark was there, and, though he could not feel it with his fingers, he could hear its crisp rustling as he fumbled for it. Try as he would, he could not clutch hold of it. And all the time, in his consciousness, was the knowledge that each instant his feet were freezing. This thought tended to put him in a panic, but he fought against it and kept calm. He pulled on his mittens with his teeth, and threshed his arms back and forth, beating his hands with all his might against his sides. He did this sitting down, and he stood up to do it; and all the while the dog sat in the snow, its wolf brush of a tail curled around warmly over its forefront, its sharp wolf ears pricked forward intently as it watched the man. And the man, as he beat and threshed with his arms and hands, felt a great surge of envy as he regarded the creature that was warm and secure in its natural covering.

After a time he was aware of the first far-away signals of sensation in his beaten fingers. The faint tingling grew stronger till it evolved into a stinging ache that was excruciating, but which the man hailed with satisfaction. He stripped the mitten from his right hand and fetched forth the birch bark. The exposed fingers were quickly going numb again. Next he brought out his bunch of sulphur matches. But the tremendous cold had already driven the life out of his fingers. In his effort to separate one match from the others, the whole bunch fell in the snow. He tried to pick it out of the snow, but failed. The dead fingers could neither touch nor clutch. He was very careful. He drove the thought of his freezing feet, and nose, and cheeks, out of his mind, devoting his whole soul to the matches. He watched, using the sense of vision in place of that touch, and when he saw his fingers on each side the bunch, he closed them—that is, he willed to close them, for the wires were down, and the fingers did not obey. He pulled the mitten on the right hand, and beat it fiercely against his knee. Then with both mittened hands, he scooped the bunch of matches, along with much snow, into his lap. Yet he was no better off.

After some manipulation he managed to get the bunch between the heels of his mittened hands. In this fashion he carried it to his mouth. The ice crackled and snapped when by a violent effort he opened his mouth. He drew the lower jaw in, curled the upper lip out of the way, and scraped the bunch with his upper teeth in order to separate a match. He succeeded in getting one, which he dropped on his lap. He was no better off. He could not pick it up. Then he devised a way. He picked it up in his teeth and scratched it on his leg. Twenty times he scratched before he succeeded in lighting it.

As it flamed he held it with his teeth to the birch bark. But the burning brimstone went up his nostrils and into his lungs, causing him to cough spasmodically. The match fell into the snow and went out.

The old-timer on Sulphur Creek was right, he thought in the moment of controlled despair that ensued: after fifty below, a man should travel with a partner. He beat his hands, but failed in exciting any sensation. Suddenly be bared both hands, removing the mittens with his teeth. He caught the whole bunch between the heels of his hands. His arm muscles not being frozen enable him to press the hand heels tightly against the matches. Then he scratched the bunch along his leg. It flared into flame, seventy sulphur matches at once! There was no wind to blow them out. He kept his head to one side to escape the strangling fumes, and held the blazing bunch to the birch bark. As he so held it, he became aware of sensation in his hand. His flesh was burning. He could smell it. Deep down below the surface he could feel it. The sensation developed into pain that grew acute. And still he endured it, holding the flame of the matches clumsily to the bark that would not light readily because his own burning hands were in the way, absorbing most of the flame.

At last, when he could endure no more, he jerked his hands apart. The blazing matches fell sizzling into the snow, but the birch bark was alight. He began laying dry grasses and the tiniest twigs on the flame. He could not pick and choose, for he had to lift the fuel between the heels of his hands. Small pieces of rotten wood and green moss clung to the twigs, and he bit them off as well as he could with his teeth. He cherished the flame carefully and awkwardly. It meant life, and it must not perish. The withdrawal of blood from the surface of his body now made him begin to shiver, and he grew more awkward. A large piece of green moss fell squarely on the little fire. He tried to poke it out with his fingers, but his shivering frame made him poke too far, and he disrupted the nucleus of the little fire, the burning grasses and tiny twigs separating and scattering. He tried to poke them together again, but in

spite of the tenseness of the effort, his shivering got away with
him, and the twigs were hopelessly scattered. Each twig
gushed a puff of smoke and went out. The fire provider had
failed. As he looked apathetically about him, his eyes chanced
on the dog, sitting across the ruins of the fire from him, in the
snow, making restless, hunching movements, slightly lifting
one forefoot and then the other, shifting its weight back and
forth on them with wistful eagerness.

The sight of the dog put a wild idea into his head. He
remembered the tale of the man, caught in a blizzard, who
killed a steer and crawled inside the carcass, and so was saved.
He would kill the dog and bury his hands in the warm body
until the numbness went out of them. Then he could build
another fire. He spoke to the dog, calling it to him; but in his
voice was a strange note of fear that frightened the animal,
who had never known the man to speak in such a way before.
Something was the matter, and its suspicious nature sensed
danger—it knew not what danger, but somewhere, somehow,
in its brain arose an apprehension of the man. It flattened its
ears down at the sound of the man's voice, and its restless,
hunching movements and the liftings and shiftings of its forefeet became more pronounced; but it would not come to the
man. He got on his hands and knees and crawled towards
the dog. This unusual posture again excited suspicion, and
the animal sidled mincingly away.

The man sat up in the snow for a moment and struggled for
calmness. Then he pulled on his mittens, by means of his
teeth, and got upon his feet. He glanced down at first in order
to assure himself that he was really standing up, for the
absence of sensation in his feet left him unrelated to the earth.
His erect position in itself started to drive the webs of suspicion
from the dog's mind; and when he spoke peremptorily, with
the sound of whip lashes in his voice, the dog rendered its
customary allegiance and came to him. As it came within
reaching distance, the man lost his control. His arms flashed
out to the dog, and he experienced genuine surprise when he
discovered that his hands could not clutch, that there was

neither bend nor feeling in the fingers. He had forgotten for the moment that they were frozen and that they were freezing more and more. All this happened quickly, and before the animal could get away, he encircled its body with his arms. He sat down in the snow, and in this fashion held the dog, while it snarled and whined and struggled.

But it was all he could do, hold its body encircled in his arms and sit there. He realized he could not kill the dog. There was no way to do it. With his helpless hands he could neither draw nor hold his sheath knife nor throttle the animal. He released it, and it plunged wildly away, with tail between its legs, and still snarling. It halted forty feet away and surveyed him curiously, with ears sharply pricked forward.

The man looked down at his hands in order to locate them, and found them hanging on the ends of his arms. It struck him as curious that one should have to use his eyes in order to find out where his hands were. He began threshing his arms back and forth, beating the mittened hands against his sides. He did this for five minutes, violently, and his heart pumped enough blood up to the surface to put a stop to his shivering. But no sensation was aroused in the hands. He had an impression that they hung like weights on the ends of his arms, but when he tried to run the impression down, he could not find it.

A certain fear of death, dull and oppressive, came to him. This fear quickly became poignant as he realized that it was no longer a mere matter of freezing his fingers and toes, or of losing his hands and feet, but that it was a matter of life and death with the chances against him. This threw him into a panic, and he turned and ran up the creek bed along the old, dim trail. The dog joined in behind him and kept up with him. He ran blindly, without intention, in fear such as he had never known in his life. Slowly, as he ploughed and floundered through the snow, he began to see things again—the banks of the creek, the old timber jams, the leafless aspens, and the sky. The running made him feel better. He did not shiver. Maybe, if he ran on, his feet would thaw out; and, anyway, if he ran far enough, he would reach camp and the boys.

Without doubt he would lose some fingers and toes and some of his face; but the boys would take care of him, and save the rest of him when he got there. And at the same time there was another thought in his mind that said he would never get to the camp and the boys; that it was too many miles away, that the freezing had too great a start on him, and that he would soon be stiff and dead. This thought he kept in the background and refused to consider. Sometimes it pushed itself forward and demanded to be heard, but he thrust it back and strove to think of other things.

It struck him as curious that he could run at all on feet so frozen that he could not feel them when they struck the earth and took the weight of his body. He seemed to himself to skim along above the surface, and to have no connection with the earth. Somewhere he had once seen a winged Mercury, and he wondered if Mercury felt as he felt when skimming over the earth.

His theory of running until he reached camp and the boys had one flaw in it: he lacked the endurance. Several times he stumbled, and finally he tottered, crumpled up, and fell. When he tried to rise, he failed. He must sit and rest, he decided, and next time he would merely walk and keep on going. As he sat and regained his breath, he noted that he was feeling quite warm and comfortable. He was not shivering, and it even seemed that a warm glow had come to his chest and trunk. And yet, when he touched his nose or cheeks, there was no sensation. Running would not thaw them out. Nor would it thaw out his hands and feet. Then the thought came to him that the frozen portions of his body must be extending. He tried to keep this thought down, to forget it, to think of something else; he was aware of the panicky feeling that it caused, and he was afraid of the panic. But the thought asserted itself, and persisted, until it produced a vision of his body totally frozen. This was too much, and he made another wild run along the trail. Once he slowed down to a walk, but the thought of the freezing extending itself made him run again.

And all the time the dog ran with him, at his heels. When he fell down a second time, it curled its tail over its forefeet and sat in front of him, facing him, curiously eager and intent. The warmth and security of the animal angered him, and he cursed it till it flattened down its ears appeasingly. This time the shivering came more quickly upon the man. He was losing in his battle with the frost. It was creeping into his body from all sides. The thought of it drove him on, but he ran no more than a hundred feet, when he staggered and pitched headlong. It was his last panic. When he had recovered his breath and control, he sat up and entertained in his mind the conception of meeting death with dignity. However, the conception did not come to him in such terms. His own idea of it was that he had been making a fool of himself, running around like a chicken with its head cut off—such was the simile that occurred to him. Well, he was bound to freeze anyway, and he might as well take it decently. With this new-found peace of mind came the first glimmerings of drowsiness. A good idea, he thought, to sleep off to death. It was like taking an anaesthetic. Freezing was not so bad as people thought. There were lots worse ways to die.

He pictured the boys finding his body next day. Suddenly he found himself with them, coming along the trail looking for himself. And, still with them, he came around a turn in the trail and found himself lying in the snow. He did not belong with himself any more, for even then he was out of himself, standing with the boys and looking at himself in the snow. It certainly was cold, was his thought. When he got back to the States he could tell the folks what real cold was. He drifted on from this to a vision of the old-timer on Sulphur Creek. He could see him quite clearly, warm and comfortable, and smoking a pipe.

'You were right, old hoss; you were right,' the man mumbled to the old-timer of Sulphur Creek.

Then the man drowsed off into what seemed to him the most comfortable and satisfying sleep he had ever known. The dog sat facing him and waiting. The brief day drew to a close

F

in a long, slow twilight. There were no signs of a fire to be made, and, besides, never in the dog's experience had it known a man to sit like that in the snow and make no fire. As the twilight drew on, its eager yearning for the fire mastered it, and with a great lifting and shifting of forefeet, it whined softly, then flattened its ears down in anticipation of being chidden by the man. But the man remained silent. Later the dog whined loudly. And still later it crept close to the man and caught the scent of death. This made the animal bristle and back away. A little longer it delayed, howling under the stars that leaped and danced and shone brightly in the cold sky. Then it turned and trotted up the trail in the direction of the camp it knew, where were the other food providers and fire providers.

The Pearls of Parlay

THE Kanaka helmsman put the wheel down and the *Malahini* slipped into the eye of the wind and righted to an even keel. Her headsails emptied; there was a rat-tat of reef points and quick shifting of boom tackles, and she heeled over and filled away on the other tack. Though it was early morning and the wind brisk the five white men who lounged on the poop deck were scantily clad. David Grief and his guest, Gregory Mulhall, an Englishman, were still in pyjamas, their naked feet thrust into Chinese slippers. The captain and mate were in thin undershirts and unstarched duck trousers, while the supercargo still held in his hands the undershirt he was reluctant to put on. The sweat stood out on his forehead and he seemed to thrust his bare chest thirstily into the wind that did not cool.

'Pretty muggy for a breeze like this,' he complained.

'And what's it doing around in the west? That's what I want to know,' was Grief's contribution to the general plaint.

'It won't last and it ain't been there long,' said Hermann, the Holland mate. 'She is been chop round all night—five minutes here, ten minutes there, one hour somewhere other quarter.'

'Something makin', something makin',' Captain Warfield croaked, spreading his bushy beard with the fingers of both hands and shoving the thatch of his chin into the breeze in a vain search for coolness. 'Weather's been crazy for a fortnight. Haven't had the proper trades in three weeks. Everything's mixed up. Barometer was pumping at sunset last night and it's pumping now, though the weather sharps say it don't mean anything. All the same, I've got a prejudice against seeing it pump. Gets on my nerves, sort of, you know. She was pumping that way the time we lost the *Lancaster*. I was only an apprentice, but I can remember that well enough. Brand-new four-masted steel ship; first voyage—broke the old man's heart.

He'd been forty years in the company. Just faded away and died the next year.'

Despite the wind and the early hour, the heat was suffocating. The wind whispered coolness but did not deliver coolness. It might have blown off the Sahara, save for the extreme humidity with which it was laden. There was no fog or mist, nor hint of fog or mist; yet the dimness of distance produced the impression.

There were no defined clouds; yet so thickly were the heavens covered by a messy cloud pall that the sun failed to shine through.

'Ready about!' Captain Warfield ordered with slow sharpness.

The brown, breechclouted Kanaka sailors moved languidly but quickly to head sheets and boom tackles.

'Hard alee!'

The helmsman ran the spokes over with no hint of gentling and the *Malahini* darted prettily into the wind and about.

'Jove! She's a witch!' was Mulhall's appreciation. 'I didn't know you South Sea traders sailed yachts.'

'She was a Gloucester fisherman originally,' Grief explained, 'and the Gloucester boats are all yachts when it comes to build, rig, and sailing.'

'But you're heading right in—why don't you make it?' came the Englishman's criticism.

'Try it, Captain Warfield,' Grief suggested. 'Show him what a lagoon entrance is on a strong ebb.'

'Close and by!' the captain ordered.

'Close and by!' the Kanaka repeated, easing half a spoke.

The *Malahini* laid squarely into the narrow passage, which was the lagoon entrance of a large, long, and narrow oval of an atoll. The atoll was shaped as if three atolls, in the course of building, had collided and coalesced and failed to rear the partition walls. Coconut palms grew in spots on the circle of sand and there were many gaps where the sand was too low to the sea for coconuts, through which could be seen the protected lagoon where the water lay flat like the ruffled surface of a mirror. Many square miles of water were in the irregular lagoon, all of which surged out on the ebb through the one narrow channel. So narrow was the channel, so large the outflow of water, that the passage was more like the rapids of a river than the mere tidal entrance to an atoll. The water boiled and whirled and swirled and drove outward in a white foam of stiff, serrated waves. Each heave and blow on her bows of the upstanding waves of the current swung the *Malahini* off the straight lead and wedged her as with wedges of steel towards the side of the passage. Part way in she was when her closeness to the coral edge compelled her to go about. On the opposite tack, broadside to the current, she swept seaward with the current's speed.

'Now's the time for that new and expensive engine of yours,' Grief jeered good-naturedly.

That the engine was a sore point with Captain Warfield was patent. He had begged and badgered for it until, in the end, Grief had given his consent.

'It will pay for itself yet,' the captain retorted. 'You wait and see. It beats insurance; and you know the underwriters won't stand for insurance in the Paumotus.'

Grief pointed to a small cutter beating up astern of them on the same course.

'I'll wager five francs the little *Nuhiva* beats us in.'

'Sure!' Captain Warfield agreed. 'She's overpowered. We're like a liner alongside of her and we've only got forty horse-power. She's got ten horse, and she's a little skimming dish. She could skate across the froth of hell; but just the same she can't buck this current. It's running ten knots right now.'

And at the rate of ten knots, buffeted and jerkily rolled, the *Malahini* went out to sea with the tide.

'She'll slacken in half an hour—then we'll make headway,' Captain Warfield said with an irritation explained by his next words. 'He has no right to call it Parlay. It's down on the Admiralty charts, and the French charts too, as Hikihoho. Bougainville discovered it and named it from the natives.'

'What's the name matter?' the supercargo demanded,

taking advantage of speech to pause with arms shoved into the sleeves of the undershirt. 'There it is, right under our nose; and old Parlay is there with the pearls.'

'Who see them pearls?' Hermann queried, looking from one to another.

'It's well known,' was the supercargo's reply. He turned to the steersman. 'Tell them, Tai-Hotauri.'

The Kanaka, pleased and self-conscious, took and gave a spoke. 'My brother dive for Parlay three-four month and he make much talk about pearl. Hikihoho very good place for pearl.'

'And the pearl buyers have never got him to part with a pearl,' the captain broke in.

'And they say the old man had a hatful for Armande when he sailed for Tahiti,' the supercargo carried on the tale.

'That's fifteen years ago and he's been adding to it ever since—stored the shell as well. Everybody's seen that—hundreds of tons of it. They say the lagoon's fished clean now. Maybe that's why he's announced the auction.'

'If he really sells what he has, this will be the biggest year's output of pearls in the Paumotus,' Grief said.

'I say, now, look here!' Mulhall burst forth, harried by the humid heat as much as the rest of them. 'What's it all about? Who's the old beachcomber anyway? What are all these pearls? Why so secretive about it?'

'Hikihoho belongs to old Parlay,' the supercargo answered. 'He's got a fortune in pearls, saved up for years and years; and he sent the word out weeks ago that he'd auction them off to the buyers tomorrow. See those schooners' masts sticking up inside the lagoon?'

'Eight—so I see,' said Hermann.

'What are they doing in a dinky atoll like this?' the supercargo went on. 'There isn't a schoonerload of copra a year in the place. They've come for the auction. That's why we're here. That's why the little *Nuhiva*'s bumping along astern there—though what she can buy is beyond me. Narii Herring —he's an English Jew half-caste—owns and runs her, and his only assets are his nerve, his debts, and his whisky bills. He's a genius in such things. He owes so much there isn't a merchant in Papeete who isn't interested in his welfare. They go out of their way to throw work in his way. They've got to—and a dandy stunt it is for Narii. Now I owe nobody. What's the result? If I fell down in a fit on the beach they'd let me lie there and die. They wouldn't lose anything. But Narii Herring! What wouldn't they do if he fell in a fit? Their best wouldn't be too good for him. They've got too much money tied up in him to let him lie. They'd take him into their homes and hand-nurse him like a brother. Let me tell you, honesty in paying bills ain't what it's cracked up to be.'

'What's this Narii chap got to do with it?' was the Englishman's short-tempered demand. And, turning to Grief, he said: 'What's all this pearl nonsense? Begin at the beginning.'

'You'll have to help me out,' Grief warned the others as he began. 'Old Parlay is a character. From what I've seen of him, I believe he's partly and mildly insane. Anyway, here's the story. Parlay's a full-blooded Frenchman. He told me once that he came from Paris. His accent is the true Parisian. He arrived down here in the old days. Went to trading and all the rest. That's how he got in on Hikihoho. Came in trading when trading was the real thing. About a hundred miserable Paumotans lived on the island. He married the Queen—native fashion. When she died everything was his. Measles came through and there weren't more than a dozen survivors. He fed them and worked them, and was King. Now before the Queen died she gave birth to a girl. That's Armande. When she was three he sent her to the convent at Papeete. When she was seven or eight he sent her to France. You begin to glimpse the situation. The best and most aristocratic convent in France was none too good for the only daughter of a Paumotan island king and capitalist—and you know the old-country French draw no colour line. She was educated like a princess and she accepted herself in much the same way. Also she thought she was all white and never dreamed of a bar sinister.

'Now comes the tragedy. The old man had always been

cranky and erratic, and he'd played the despot on Hikihoho
so long that he'd got the idea in his head that there was
nothing wrong with the King—or the princess either. When
Armande was eighteen he sent for her. He had slews and
slathers of money, as Yankee Bill would say. He'd built the
big house on Hikihoho and a whacking fine bungalow in
Papeete. She was to arrive on the mail boat from New Zealand
and he sailed in his schooner to meet her at Papeete. And he
might have carried the situation off, despite the hens and bull
beasts of Papeete, if it hadn't been for the hurricane. That was
the year, wasn't it, when Manu-Huni was swept and eleven
hundred drowned?'

The others nodded and Captain Warfield said: 'I was in
the *Magpie* that blow and we went ashore, all hands and the
cook—*Magpie* and all—a quarter of a mile into the coconuts
at the head of Taiohae Bay—and it a supposedly hurricane-
proof harbour.'

'Well,' Grief continued, 'old Parlay got caught in the same
blow and arrived in Papeete with his hatful of pearls three
weeks too late. He'd had to jack up his schooner and build
half a mile of ways before he could get her back into the
sea.

'Meantime there was Armande at Papeete. Nobody called
on her. She did, French fashion, make the initial calls on the
governor and the port doctor. They saw her, but neither of
their hen wives was at home to her or returned the call. She
was out of caste—without caste—though she had never
dreamed it; and that was the gentle way they broke the infor-
mation to her. There was a gay young lieutenant on the French
cruiser. He lost his heart to her, but not his head. You can
imagine the shock to this young woman, refined, beautiful,
raised like an aristocrat, pampered with the best of old France
that money could buy! And you can guess the end.' He shrugged his shoulders. 'There was a Japanese servant in the bungalow. He saw it—said she did it with the proper spirit of the
samurai. Took a stiletto—no thrust, no drive, no wild rush for
annihilation—took the stiletto, placed the point carefully

against her heart, and with both hands slowly and steadily pressed home.

'Old Parlay arrived after that with his pearls. There was one single one of them, they say, worth sixty thousand francs. Peter Gee saw it and has told me he offered that much for it. The old man went clean off for a while. They had him strait-jacketed in the Colonial Club for two days——'

'His wife's uncle, an old Paumotan, cut him out of the jacket and turned him loose,' the supercargo corroborated.

'And then old Parlay proceeded to eat things up,' Grief went on. 'Pumped three bullets into the scalawag of a lieu-tenant——'

'Who lay in sick bay for three months,' Captain Warfield contributed.

'Flung a glass of wine in the governor's face; fought a duel with the port doctor; beat up his native servants, wrecked the hospital; broke two ribs and the collar-bone of a man nurse—and escaped; went down to his schooner, a gun in each hand, daring the chief of police and all the gendarmes to arrest him, and sailed for Hikihoho. And they say he's never left the island since.'

The supercargo nodded. 'That was fifteen years ago, and he's never budged.'

'And added to his pearls,' said the captain. 'He's a blithering old lunatic. Makes my flesh creep. He's a regular Finn.'

'What's that?' Mulhall asked.

'Bosses the weather—that's what the natives believe, at any rate. Ask Tai-Hotauri there. Hey, Tai-Hotauri, what you think old Parlay do along weather?'

'Just the same one big weather devil!' came the Kanaka's answer. 'I know. He want big blow, he make big blow. He want no wind, no wind come.'

'A regular old warlock,' said Mulhall.

'No good luck, them pearl,' Tai-Hotauri blurted out, rolling his head ominously. 'He say he sell. Plenty schooner come. Then he make big hurricane; everybody finish, you see. All native men say so.'

'It's hurricane season now,' Captain Warfield laughed morosely. 'They're not far wrong. It's making for something right now; and I'd feel better if the *Malahini* was a thousand miles away from here.'

'He is a bit mad,' Grief concluded. 'I've tried to get his point of view. It's—well, it's mixed. For eighteen years he'd centred everything on Armande. Half the time he believes she's still alive—not yet come back from France. That's one of the reasons he held on to the pearls. And all the time he hates white men. He never forgets they killed her, though a great deal of the time he forgets she's dead.'

'Hello! Where's your wind?'

The sails bellied emptily overhead and Captain Warfield grunted his disgust. Intolerable as the heat had been, in the absence of wind it was almost overpowering. The sweat oozed out on all their faces; and now one and then another drew deep breaths, involuntarily questing for more air.

'Here she comes again—an eight-point haul! Boom tackles across! Jump!'

The Kanakas sprang to the captain's orders and for five minutes the schooner laid directly into the passage—and even gained on the current. Again the breeze fell flat, then puffed from the old quarter, compelling a shift back of sheets and tackles.

'Here comes the *Nuhiva*,' Grief said. 'She's got her engine on. Look at her skim!'

'All ready?' the captain asked the engineer, a Portuguese half-caste, whose head and shoulders protruded from the small hatch just for'ard of the cabin, and who wiped the dripping sweat from his face with a bunch of greasy waste.

'Sure!' he replied.

'Then let her go!'

The engineer disappeared into his den and a moment later the exhaust muffler coughed and sputtered overside; but the schooner could not hold her lead. The little cutter travelled three feet to her two and was quickly alongside and forging ahead.

Only natives were on her deck and the man who was steering waved his hand in derisive greeting and farewell.

'That's Narii Herring,' Grief told Mulhall, 'the big fellow at the wheel—the nerviest and most conscienceless scoundrel in the Paumotus.'

Five minutes later a cry of joy from their own Kanakas centred all eyes on the *Nuhiva*. Her engine had broken down and they were overtaking her. The *Malahini*'s sailors sprang into the rigging and jeered as they went by; the little cutter, heeled over by the wind, was going backward on the tide.

'Some engine, that of ours!' Grief approved as the lagoon opened before them and the course was changed across it to the anchorage.

Captain Warfield was visibly cheered, though he merely grunted: 'It'll pay for itself; never fear.'

The *Malahini* ran well into the centre of the little fleet ere she found swinging room to anchor.

'There's Isaacs on the *Dolly*,' Grief observed with a hand-wave of greeting. 'And Peter Gee's on the *Roberta*. Couldn't keep him away from a pearl sale like this. And there's Francini on the *Cactus*. They're all here—all the buyers. Old Parlay will surely get a price.'

'They haven't repaired the engine yet,' Captain Warfield grumbled gleefully. He was looking across the lagoon to where the *Nuhiva*'s sails showed through the sparse coconuts.

II

The house of Parlay was a big two-storey frame affair, built of California lumber, with a galvanized iron roof. So disproportionate was it to the slender ring of the atoll that it showed out upon the sand strip and above it like some monstrous excrescence. They of the *Malahini* paid the courtesy visit ashore immediately after anchoring. Other captains and buyers were in the big room examining the pearls that were to be auctioned next day. Paumotan servants, natives of Hikihoho and relatives of the owner, moved about, dispensing whisky and absinthe.

And through the curious company moved Parlay himself, cackling and sneering, the withered wreck of what had once been a tall and powerful man. His eyes were deep-sunken and feverish, his cheeks fallen in and cavernous. The hair of his head seemed to have come out in patches and his moustache and imperial had been shed in the same lopsided way.

'Jove!' Mulhall muttered under his breath. 'A long-legged Napoleon III—but burnt out, baked, and fire-crackled. And mangy! No wonder he crooks his head to one side. He's got to keep the balance.'

'Goin' to have a blow,' was the old man's greeting to Grief. 'You must think a lot of pearls to come a day like this.'

'They're worth going to inferno for,' Grief laughed genially back, running his eyes over the surface of the table covered by the display.

'Other men have already made that journey for them,' old Parlay cackled. 'See this one!' He pointed to a large, perfect pearl, the size of a small walnut, that lay apart on a piece of chamois. 'They offered me sixty thousand francs for it in Tahiti. They'll bid as much and more for it tomorrow if they aren't blown away. Well, that pearl was found by my cousin— my cousin by marriage. He was a native, you see. Also he was a thief. He hid it. It was mine. His cousin, who was also my cousin—we're all related here—killed him for it and fled away in a cutter to Noo-Nau. I pursued; but the chief of Noo-Nau had killed him for it before I got there. Oh yes, there are many dead men represented on the table there. Have a drink, Captain? Your face is not familiar. You are new in the islands?'

'It's Captain Robinson, of the *Roberta*,' Grief said, introducing them.

Meantime Mulhall had shaken hands with Peter Gee.

'I never fancied there were so many pearls in the world,' Mulhall said.

'Nor have I ever seen so many together at one time,' Peter Gee admitted.

'What ought they to be worth?' asked Mulhall.

'Fifty or sixty thousand pounds—and that's to us buyers. In Paris . . .' He shrugged his shoulders.

Mulhall wiped the sweat from his eyes. All were sweating profusely and breathing hard. There was no ice, and the whisky and absinthe went down lukewarm.

'Yes, yes!' Parlay was cackling. 'Many dead men lie on the table there. I know those pearls, all of them. You see those three—perfectly matched, aren't they? A diver from Easter Island got them for me inside a week. Next week a shark got him—took his arm off and blood poison did the business. And that big baroque there—nothing much; if I'm offered twenty francs for it tomorrow I'll be in luck—it came out of twenty-two fathoms of water. The man was from Rarotonga. He broke all diving records. He got it out of twenty-two fathoms. I saw him. And he burst his lungs at the same time, or got the bends; for he died in two hours. He died screaming. They could hear him for miles. He was the most powerful native I ever saw. Half a dozen of my divers have died of the bends. And more men will die—more men will die!'

'Oh, hush your croaking, Parlay!' chided one of the captains. 'It ain't going to blow.'

'If I was a strong young man I couldn't get up hook and get out fast enough,' the old man retorted in the falsetto of age. 'Not if I was a strong young man with the taste for wine yet in my mouth. But not you. You'll all stay. I wouldn't advise you if I thought you'd go. You can't drive buzzards away from the carrion. Have another drink, my brave sailormen. Well, well! What men will dare for a few little oyster drops! There they are, the beauties! Auction tomorrow at ten sharp. Old Parlay's selling out and the buzzards are gathering—old Parlay, who was a stronger man in his day than any of them and who will see most of them dead yet!'

'If he isn't a vile old beast!' the supercargo of the *Malahin* whispered to Peter Gee.

'What if she does blow?' said the captain of the *Dolly*, 'Hikihoho's never been swept.'

'The more reason she will be, then,' Captain Warfield answered back. 'I wouldn't trust her.'

'Who's croaking now?' Grief reproved.

'I'd hate to lose that new engine before it paid for itself,' Captain Warfield replied gloomily.

Parlay skipped with astonishing nimbleness across the crowded room to where a ship's barometer hung on the wall.

'Take a look, my brave sailormen!' he cried exultantly.

The man nearest read the glass. The sobering effect showed plainly on his face.

'It's dropped ten,' was all he said, yet every face went anxious and there was a restlessness as if every man desired immediately to start for the door.

'Listen!' Parlay commanded.

In the silence the outer surf seemed to have become unusually loud. There was a great, rumbling roar.

'A big sea is beginning to set,' someone said; and there was a movement to the windows, where all gathered.

Through the sparse coconuts they gazed seaward. An orderly succession of huge, smooth seas was rolling down upon the coral shore. For some minutes they gazed on the strange sight and talked in low voices, and in those few minutes it was manifest to all that the waves were increasing in size. It was uncanny, this rising sea in a dead calm, and their voices unconsciously sank lower. Old Parlay shocked them with his abrupt cackle.

'There is yet time to get away to sea, brave gentlemen. You can tow across the lagoon with your whaleboats.'

'It's all right, old man,' said Darling, the mate of the *Cactus*, a stalwart youngster of twenty-five. 'The blow's to the south'ard and passing on. We'll not get a whiff of it.'

An air of relief went through the room. Conversations were started, and the voices became louder. Several of the buyers even went back to the table to continue the examination of the pearls. Parlay's cackle rose higher.

'That's right,' he encouraged. 'If the world was coming to an end you'd go on buying.'

'We'll buy these tomorrow,' Isaacs assured him.

'Then you'll be doing your buying in hell!'

The chorus of incredulous laughter incensed the old man. He turned fiercely on Darling.

'Since when have children like you come to the knowledge of storms? And who is the man who has plotted the hurricane courses of the Paumotus? What books will you find it in? I sailed the Paumotus before the oldest of you drew breath. I know! To the eastward the paths of the hurricanes are on so wide a circle they make a straight line. To the westward here they make a sharp curve. Remember your chart. How did it happen the hurricane of '91 swept Auri and Hiolau? The curve, my brave boy, the curve! In an hour, or two or three at most, will come the wind. Listen to that!'

A vast, rumbling crash shook the coral foundations of the atoll. The house quivered to it. The native servants, with bottles of whisky and absinthe in their hands, shrank together as if for protection and stared with fear through the windows at the mighty wash of the wave lapping far up the beach to the corner of a copra shed.

Parlay looked at the barometer, giggled, and leered around at his guests. Captain Warfield strode across to see.

'Twenty-nine seventy-five!' he read. 'She's gone down five more. The old devil's right. She's a-coming—and it's me, for one, for aboard!'

'It's growing dark,' Isaacs half whimpered.

'Jove! It's like a stage,' Mulhall said to Grief, looking at his watch. 'Ten o'clock in the morning and it's like twilight. Down go the lights for the tragedy. Where's the slow music?'

In answer another rumbling crash shook the atoll and the house. Almost in a panic the company started for the door. In the dim light their sweaty faces appeared ghastly. Isaacs panted asthmatically in the suffocating heat.

'What's your haste?' Parlay chuckled and girded at his departing guests. 'A last drink, brave gentlemen!' No one noticed him. As they took the shell-bordered path to the beach he stuck his head out at the door and called: 'Don't forget, gentlemen—at ten tomorrow old Parlay sells his pearls!'

III

On the beach a curious scene took place. Whaleboat after whaleboat was being hurriedly manned and shoved off. It had grown still darker. The stagnant calm continued and the sand shook under their feet with each buffet of the sea on the outer shore. Narii Herring walked leisurely along the sand. He grinned at the very evident haste of the captains and buyers. With him were three of his Kanakas and also Tai-Hotauri.

'Get into the boat and take an oar,' Captain Warfield ordered the latter.

Tai-Hotauri came over jauntily, while Narii Herring and his Kanakas paused and looked on from forty feet away.

'I work no more for you, skipper,' Tai-Hotauri said insolently and loudly; but his face belied his words, for he was guilty of a prodigious wink. 'Fire me, skipper,' he huskily whispered with a second significant wink.

Captain Warfield took the cue and proceeded to do some acting himself. He raised his fist and his voice.

'Get into that boat, you swine,' he thundered, 'or I'll knock seven bells out of you!'

The Kanaka drew back truculently and Grief stepped between to placate his captain.

'I go to work on the *Nuhiva*,' Tai-Hotauri said, rejoining the other group.

'Come back here!' the captain threatened.

'He's a free man, skipper,' Narii Herring spoke up. 'He's sailed with me in the past and he's sailing with me again—that's all.'

'Come on; we must get on board,' Grief urged. 'Look how dark it's getting!'

Captain Warfield gave in, but as the boat shoved off he stood up in the stern sheets and shook his fist ashore.

'I'll settle with you yet, Narii!' he cried. 'You're the only skipper in the group who steals other men's sailors.' He sat down and in a lowered voice queried: 'Now what's Tai-Hotauri up to? He's on to something; but what is it?'

IV

As the boat came alongside the *Malahini*, Hermann's anxious face greeted them over the rail.

'Bottom fall out from barometer,' he announced. 'She's goin' to blow. I got starboard anchor overhaul.'

'Overhaul the big one too,' Captain Warfield ordered, taking charge. 'And here, some of you, hoist in this boat. Lower her down to the deck and lash her, bottom up.'

Men were busy at work on the decks of all the schooners. There was a great clanking of chains being overhauled; and now one craft and now another hove in, veered, and dropped a second anchor.

Like the *Malahini*, those that had third anchors were preparing to drop them when the wind showed what quarter it was to blow from.

The roar of the big surf continually grew, though the lagoon lay in mirrorlike calm. There was no sign of life where Parlay's big house perched on the sand. Boat and copra sheds and the sheds where the shell was stored were deserted.

'For two cents I'd up anchors and get out,' Grief said. 'I'd do it anyway if it were open sea; but those chains of atolls to the north and east have us pocketed. We've a better chance right there. What do you think, Captain Warfield?'

'I agree with you, though a lagoon is no millpond for riding it out. I wonder where she's going to start from? Hello! There goes one of Parlay's copra sheds!'

They could see the grass-thatched shed lift and collapse, while a froth of foam cleared the crest of the sand and ran down to the lagoon.

'Breached across!' Mulhall exclaimed. 'That's something for a starter. There she comes again!'

The wreck of the shed was now flung up and left on the sand crest. A third wave buffeted it into fragments, which washed down the slope towards the lagoon.

'If she blow I would as be cooler yet,' Hermann grunted. 'No longer can I breathe. It is damn hot. I am dry like a stove.'

He chopped open a drinking coconut with his heavy sheath knife and drained the contents. The rest of them followed his example, pausing once to watch one of Parlay's shell sheds go down in ruin. The barometer now registered 29·50.

'Must be pretty close to the centre of the area of low pressure,' Grief remarked cheerfully. 'I was never through the eye of a hurricane before. It will be an experience for you too, Mulhall. From the speed the barometer's dropped it's going to be a big one.'

Captain Warfield groaned, and all eyes were drawn to him. He was looking through the glasses down the length of the lagoon to the south-east.

'There she comes,' he said quietly.

They did not need glasses to see. A flying film, strangely marked, seemed drawing over the surface of the lagoon. Abreast of it, along the atoll, travelling with equal speed, was a stiff bending of the coconut palms and a blur of flying leaves. The front of the wind on the water was a solid, sharply defined strip of dark-coloured, wind-vexed water. In advance of this strip, like skirmishers, were flashes of windflaws. Behind this strip, a quarter of a mile in width, was a strip of what seemed glassy calm. Next came another dark strip of wind—and behind that the lagoon was all crisping, boiling whiteness.

'What is that calm streak?' Mulhall asked.

'Calm,' Warfield answered.

'But it travels as fast as the wind,' was the other's objection.

'It has to, or it would be overtaken and there wouldn't be any calm. It's a double-header. I saw a big squall like that off Savaii once. A regular double-header. Smash! It hit us; then it lulled to nothing and smashed us a second time. Stand by and hold on. Here she is on top of us. Look at the *Roberta*!'

The *Roberta*, lying nearest to the wind at slack chains, was swept off broadside like a straw. Then her chains brought her up, bow on to the wind, with an astonishing jerk. Schooner after schooner—the *Malahini* with them—was now sweeping away with the first gust and fetching up on taut chains.

Mulhall and several of the Kanakas were taken off their feet when the *Malahini* jerked to her anchor.

And then there was no wind. The flying calm streak had reached them. Grief lighted a match and the unshielded flame burned without flickering in the still air. A very dim twilight prevailed. The cloud-sky, lowering as it had been for hours, seemed now to have descended quite down upon the sea.

The *Roberta* tightened to her chains when the second head of the hurricane hit, as did schooner after schooner in swift succession. The sea, white with fury, boiled in tiny, spitting wavelets. The deck of the *Malahini* vibrated under their feet. The taut-stretched halyards beat a tattoo against the masts, and all the rigging, as if smitten by some mighty hand, set up a wild thrumming. It was impossible to face the wind and breathe. Mulhall, crouching with the others behind the shelter of the cabin, discovered this; and his lungs were filled in an instant with so great a volume of driven air which he could not expel that he nearly strangled ere he could turn his head away.

'It's incredible!' he gasped; but no one heard him.

Hermann and several Kanakas were crawling for'ard on hands and knees to let go the third anchor. Grief touched Captain Warfield and pointed to the *Roberta*. She was dragging down upon them. Warfield put his mouth to Grief's ear and shouted:

'We're dragging too!'

Grief sprang to the wheel and put it hard over, veering the *Malahini* to port. The third anchor took hold and the *Roberta* went by, stern first, a dozen yards away. They waved their hands to Peter Gee and Captain Robinson, who, with a number of sailors, were at work on the bow.

'He's knocking out the shackles!' Grief shouted. 'Going to chance the passage! Got to! Anchors skating!'

'We're holding now!' came the answering shout. 'There goes the *Cactus* down on the *Misi*. That settles them!'

The *Misi* had been holding, but the added windage of the *Cactus* was too much and the entangled schooners slid away across the boiling white. Their men could be seen chopping and fighting to get them apart. The *Roberta*, cleared of her anchors, with a patch of tarpaulin set for'ard, was heading for the passage at the north-western end of the lagoon. They saw her make it and drive out to sea. The *Misi* and the *Cactus*, however, unable to get clear of each other, went ashore on the atoll half a mile from the passage.

The wind merely increased on itself and continued to increase. To face the full blast of it required all one's strength, and several minutes of crawling on deck against it tired a man to exhaustion. Hermann, with his Kanakas, plodded steadily, lashing and making secure, putting ever more gaskets on the sails. The wind ripped and tore their thin undershirts from their backs. They moved slowly, as if their bodies weighed tons, never releasing a handhold until another had been secured. Loose ends of rope stood out stiffly horizontal, and after whipping the loose ends frazzled and blew away.

Mulhall touched one and then another and pointed to the shore. The grass sheds had disappeared and Parlay's house rocked drunkenly. Because the wind blew lengthwise along the atoll the house had been sheltered by the miles of coconut trees; but the big seas, breaking across from outside, were undermining it and hammering it to pieces. Already tilted down the slope of sand, its end was imminent. Here and there in the coconut trees people had lashed themselves. The trees did not sway or thresh about. Bent over rigidly by the wind, they remained in that position and vibrated monstrously. Underneath, across the sand, surged the white spume of the breakers.

A big sea was likewise making down the length of the lagoon. It had plenty of room to kick up in the ten-mile stretch from the windward rim of the atoll, and all the schooners were bucking and plunging into it. The *Malahini* had begun shoving her bow and fo'c'sle head under the bigger ones, and at times her waist was filled rail-high with water.

'Now's the time for your engine!' Grief bellowed; and Captain Warfield, crawling over to where the engineer lay, shouted emphatic commands.

Under the engine, going full speed ahead, the *Malahini* behaved better. Though she continued to ship seas over her bow, she was not jerked down so fiercely by her anchors. On the other hand, she was unable to get any slack in the chains. The best her forty horsepower could do was to ease the strain.

Still the wind increased. The little *Nuhiva*, lying abreast of the *Malahini* and closer in to the beach, her engine still unrepaired and her captain ashore, was having a bad time of it. She buried herself so frequently and so deeply that they wondered each time if she could clear herself of the water.

At three in the afternoon, buried by a second sea before she could free herself of the preceding one, she did not come up.

Mulhall looked at Grief.

'Burst in her hatches!' was the bellowed answer.

Captain Warfield pointed to the *Winifred*, a little schooner plunging and burying outside of them, and shouted in Grief's ear. His voice came in patches of dim words, with intervals of silence when whisked away by the roaring wind.

'Rotten little tub! . . . Anchors hold. . . . But how she holds together! . . . Old as the ark.'

An hour later Hermann pointed to her. Her for'ard bits, foremast, and most of her bow were gone, having been jerked out of her by her anchors. She swung broadside, rolling in the trough and settling by the head; and in this plight she was swept away to leeward.

Five vessels now remained, and of them the *Malahini* was the only one with an engine. Fearing either the *Nuhiva*'s or the *Mildred*'s fate, two of them followed the *Roberta*'s example, knocking out the chain shackles and running for the passage. The *Dolly* was the first, but her tarpaulin was carried away and she went to destruction on the lee rim of the atoll, near the

Misi and the *Cactus*. Undeterred by this, the *Moana* let go and followed with the same result.

'Pretty good engine that, eh?' Captain Warfield yelled to his owner.

Grief put out his hand and shook. 'She's paying for herself!' he yelled back. 'The wind's shifting round to the south'ard and we ought to lie easier!'

Slowly and steadily, but with ever-increasing velocity, the wind veered round to the south and the south-west, till the three schooners that were left pointed directly in towards the beach. The wreck of Parlay's house was picked up, hurled into the lagoon, and blown out upon them. Passing the *Malahini*, it crashed into the *Papara*, lying a quarter of a mile astern. There was wild work for'ard on her and in a quarter of an hour the house went clear, but it had taken the *Papara*'s foremast and bowsprit with it.

Inshore, on their port bow, lay the *Tahaa*, slim and yacht-like, but excessively oversparred. Her anchors still held, but her captain, finding no abatement in the wind, proceeded to reduce windage by chopping down his masts.

'Pretty good engine that!' Grief congratulated his skipper. 'It will save our sticks for us yet.'

Captain Warfield shook his head dubiously.

The sea on the lagoon went swiftly down with the change of wind, but they were beginning to feel the heave and lift of the outer sea breaking across the atoll. There were not so many trees remaining. Some had been broken short off, others up-rooted. One tree they saw snapped off half-way up, three persons clinging to it, and whirled away by the wind into the lagoon. Two detached themselves from it and swam to the *Tahaa*. Not long after, just before darkness, they saw a man jump overboard from that schooner's stern and strike out strongly for the *Malahini* through the white, spitting wavelets.

'It's Tai-Hotauri,' was Grief's judgement. 'Now we'll have the news.'

The Kanaka caught the bobstay, climbed over the bow, and crawled aft. Time was given him to breathe and then, behind the part shelter of the cabin, in broken snatches and largely by signs he told his story:

'Narii . . . Damn robber! . . . He want steal . . . pearls. . . . Kill Parlay. . . . One man kill Parlay. . . . No man know what man. . . . Three Kanakas, Narii, me . . . five beans . . . hat. . . . Narii say one bean black. . . . Nobody know. . . . Kill Parlay. . . . Narii damn liar. . . . All beans black. . . . Five black. . . . Copra shed dark. . . . Every man get black bean. . . . Big wind come . . . no chance. . . . Everybody get up tree. . . . No good luck, them pearls, I tell you before . . . no good luck.'

'Where's Parlay?' Grief shouted.

'Up tree. . . . Three of his Kanakas same tree; Narii and one Kanaka 'nother tree. . . . My tree blow to hell; then I come on board.'

'Where are the pearls?'

'Up tree along Parlay. Mebbe Narii get them pearl yet.'

In the ear of one after another Grief shouted Tai-Hotauri's story. Captain Warfield was particularly incensed and they could see him grinding his teeth.

Hermann went below and returned with a riding light, but the moment it was lifted above the level of the cabin wall the wind blew it out. He had better success with the binnacle lamp, which was lighted only after many collective attempts.

'A fine night of wind,' Grief yelled in Mulhall's ear, 'and blowing harder all the time!'

'How hard?'

'A hundred miles an hour—two hundred! I don't know. Harder than I've ever seen it.'

The lagoon grew more and more troubled by the sea that swept across the atoll. Hundreds of leagues of ocean were being backed up by the hurricane, which more than overcame the lowering effect of the ebb tide. Immediately the tide began to rise, the increase in the size of the seas was noticeable. Moon and wind were heaping the South Pacific on Hikihoho atoll.

Captain Warfield returned from one of his periodical trips

to the engine room with the word that the engineer lay in a faint.

'Can't let that engine stop!' he concluded helplessly.

'All right!' Grief shouted. 'Bring him on deck. I'll spell him.'

The hatch to the engine room was battened down, access being gained through a narrow passage from the cabin. The heat and gas fumes were stifling. Grief made one hasty, comprehensive examination of the engine and the fittings of the tiny room, then blew out the oil lamp. After that he worked in darkness, save for the glow from endless cigars that he went into the cabin to light. Even-tempered as he was, he soon began to give evidences of the strain of being pent in with a mechanical monster that toiled and sobbed and slubbered in the shouting dark. Naked to the waist, covered with grease and oil, bruised and skinned from being knocked about by the plunging, jumping vessel, his head swimming from the mixture of gas and air he was compelled to breathe, he laboured on hour after hour, by turns petting, blessing, nursing, and cursing the engine and all its parts. The ignition began to go bad. The feed grew worse and, worst of all, the cylinders began to heat. In a consultation held in the cabin the half-caste engineer begged and pleaded to stop the engine for half an hour in order to cool it and to attend to the water circulation.

Captain Warfield was against any stopping. The half-caste swore that the engine would ruin itself and stop anyway, and for good. Grief, with glaring eyes, greasy and battered, yelled and cursed them both down and issued commands. Mulhall, the supercargo, and Hermann were set to work in the cabin at double-straining and triple-straining the gasoline.

A hole was chopped through the engine-room floor and a Kanaka heaved bilge water over the cylinders, while Grief continued to souse the running parts in oil.

'Didn't know you were a gasoline expert,' Captain Warfield admired when Grief came into the cabin to catch a breath of little less impure air.

'I bathe in gasoline,' he grated savagely through his teeth. 'I eat it.'

What other uses he might have found for it were never given, for at that moment all the men in the cabin, as well as the gasoline that was being strained, were smashed for'ard against the bulkhead as the *Malahini* took an abrupt, deep dive. For the space of several minutes, unable to gain their feet, they rolled back and forth and pounded and hammered from wall to wall. The schooner, swept by three big seas, creaked and groaned and quivered and, from the weight of water on her decks, behaved loggily. Grief crept to the engine, while Captain Warfield awaited his chance to get through the companionway and out on deck.

It was half an hour before he came back.

'Whaleboat's gone!' he reported. 'Galley's gone! Everything gone except the deck and hatches! And if that engine hadn't been going we'd be gone! Keep up the good work!'

By midnight the engineer's lungs and head had been sufficiently cleared of gas fumes to let him relieve Grief, who went on deck to get his own head and lungs clear. He joined the others, who crouched behind the cabin, holding on with their hands and made doubly secure by rope lashings. It was a complicated huddle, for it was the only place of refuge for the Kanakas. Some of them had accepted the skipper's invitation into the cabin, but had been driven out by the fumes. The *Malahini* was being plunged down and swept frequently, and what they breathed was air and spray and water commingled.

'Making heavy weather of it, Mulhall!' Grief yelled to his guest between immersions.

Mulhall, strangling and choking, could only nod. The scuppers could not carry off the burden of water on the schooner's deck. She rolled it out and took it in over one rail and the other; and at times, nose thrown skyward, sitting down on her heel, she avalanched it aft. It surged along the poop gangways, poured over the top of the cabin, submerging and bruising those who clung on, and went out over the stern rail.

Mulhall saw him first and drew Grief's attention. It was

Narii Herring, crouching and holding on where the dim binnacle light shone upon him. He was quite naked, save for a belt and a bare-bladed knife thrust between it and the skin.

Captain Warfield untied his lashings and made his way over the bodies of the others. When his face became visible in the light from the binnacle it was working with anger. They could see him shout, but the wind tore the sound away. He would not put his lips to Narii's ear. Instead he pointed over the side. Narii Herring understood. His white teeth showed in an amused and sneering smile, and he stood up—a magnificent figure of a man.

'It's murder!' Mulhall yelled to Grief.

'He'd have murdered old Parlay!' Grief yelled back.

For the moment the poop was clear of water and the *Malahini* on an even keel. Narii made a bravado attempt to walk to the rail, but was flung down by the wind. Thereafter he crawled, disappearing in the darkness, though there was certitude in all of them that he had gone over the side. The *Malahini* dived deep; and when they emerged from the flood that swept aft Grief got Mulhall's ear.

'Can't lose him! He's the Fish Man of Tahiti! He'll cross the lagoon and land on the other rim of the atoll—if there's any atoll left.'

Five minutes afterwards, in another submergence, a mess of bodies poured down on them over the top of the cabin. These they seized and held till the water cleared, when they carried them below and learned their identity. Old Parlay lay on his back on the floor with closed eyes and without movement. The other two were his Kanaka cousins. All three were naked and bloody. The arm of one Kanaka hung helpless and broken at his side. The other Kanaka bled freely from a hideous scalp wound.

'Narii did that?' Mulhall demanded. Grief shook his head. 'No; it's from being smashed along the deck and over the house!'

Something suddenly ceased, leaving them all in dizzying

uncertainty. For a moment it was hard to realize there was no wind. With the absolute abruptness of a sword slash the wind had been chopped off. The schooner rolled and plunged, fetching up on her anchors with a crash that for the first time they could hear. Also, for the first time, they could hear the water washing about on deck. The engineer threw off the propeller and eased the engine down.

'We're in the dead centre,' Grief said. 'Now for the shift. It will come as hard as ever.' He looked at the barometer. 'Twenty-nine thirty-two,' he read.

Not in a moment could he tone down the voice which for hours had shouted against the wind, and so loudly did he speak that, in the quiet, it hurt the others' ears.

'All his ribs are smashed,' the supercargo said, feeling along Parlay's side. 'He's still breathing; but he's a goner.'

Old Parlay groaned, moved one arm impotently, and opened his eyes. In them was the light of recognition.

'My brave gentlemen,' he whispered haltingly, 'don't forget . . . the auction . . . at ten o'clock . . . in hell!'

His eyes drooped shut and the lower jaw threatened to drop, but he mastered the qualms of dissolution long enough to emit one final, loud, derisive cackle.

Above and below pandemonium broke out. The old familiar roar of the wind was with them. The *Malahini*, caught broadside, was pressed down almost on her beam-ends as she swung the arc compelled by her anchors. They rounded her into the wind, where she jerked to an even keel. The propeller was thrown on and the engine took up its work again.

'North-west!' Captain Warfield shouted to Grief when he came on deck. 'Hauled eight points like a shot!'

'Narii'll never get across the lagoon now!' Grief observed.

'Then he'll blow back to our side—worse luck!'

V

After the passing of the centre the barometer began to rise. Equally rapid was the fall of the wind. When it was no more than a howling gale the engine lifted up in the air, parted its bedplates with a last convulsive effort of its forty horsepower, and lay down on its side. A wash of water from the bilge sizzled over it and the steam rose in clouds.

The engineer wailed his dismay, but Grief glanced over the wreck affectionately and went into the cabin to swab the grease off his chest and arms with bunches of cotton waste.

The sun was up and the gentlest of summer breezes blowing when he came on deck, after sewing up the scalp of one Kanaka and setting the other's arm. The *Malahini* lay close to the beach. For'ard, Hermann and the crew were heaving in and straightening out the tangle of anchors.

The *Papara* and the *Tahaa* were gone; and Captain Warfield, through the glasses, was searching the opposite rim of the atoll.

'Not a stick left of them,' he said. 'That's what comes of not having engines. They must have dragged across before the big shift came.'

Ashore, where Parlay's house had been, was no vestige of any house. For the space of three hundred yards, where the sea had breached, no tree or even stump was left. Here and there, farther along, stood an occasional palm, and there were numbers which had been snapped off above the ground.

In the crown of one surviving palm Tai-Hotauri asserted he saw something move. There were no boats left to the *Malahini*, and they watched him swim ashore and climb the tree.

When he came back they helped over the rail a young native girl of Parlay's household. But first she passed up to them a battered basket. In it was a litter of blind kittens—all dead save one that feebly mewed and staggered on awkward legs.

'Hello!' said Mulhall. 'Who's that?'

Along the beach they saw a man walking. He moved casually, as if out for a morning stroll. Captain Warfield gritted his teeth. It was Narii Herring.

'Hello, Skipper,' Narii called when he was abreast of them. 'Can I come aboard and get some breakfast?'

Captain Warfield's face and neck began to swell and turn purple. He tried to speak, but choked.

'For two cents . . . ! For two cents . . . !' was all he could manage to articulate.

The Law of Life

OLD Koskoosh listened greedily. Though his sight had long since faded, his hearing was still acute, and the slightest sound penetrated to the glimmering intelligence which yet abode behind the withered forehead, but which no longer gazed forth upon the things of the world. Ah! that was Sit-cum-to-ha, shrilly anathematizing the dogs as she cuffed and beat them into the harness. Sit-cum-to-ha was his daughter's daughter, but she was too busy to waste a thought upon her broken grandfather, sitting alone there in the snow, forlorn and helpless. Camp must be broken. The long trail waited while the short day refused to linger. Life called her, and the duties of life, not death. And he was very close to death now.

The thought made the old man panicky for the moment, and he stretched forth a palsied hand which wandered tremblingly over the small heap of dry wood beside him. Reassured that it was indeed there, his hand returned to the shelter of his mangy furs, and he again fell to listening. The sulky crackling of half-frozen hides told him that the chief's moose-skin lodge had been struck, and even then was being rammed and jammed into portable compass. The chief was his son, stalwart and strong, head man of the tribesmen, and a mighty hunter. As the women toiled with the camp luggage, his voice rose, chiding them for their slowness. Old Koskoosh strained his ears. It was the last time he would hear that voice. There went Geehow's lodge! And Tusken's! Seven, eight, nine; only the shaman's could be still standing. There! They were at work upon it now. He could hear the shaman grunt as he piled it on the sled. A child whimpered, and a woman soothed it with soft, crooning gutturals. Little Koo-tee, the old man thought, a fretful child, and not overstrong. It would die soon, perhaps, and they would burn a hole through the frozen tundra and pile rocks above to keep the wolverines away. Well, what did it matter? A few years at best, and as many an empty belly as a full one. And in the end, Death waited, ever-hungry and hungriest of them all.

What was that? Oh, the men lashing the sleds and drawing tight the thongs. He listened, who would listen no more. The whip-lashes snarled and bit among the dogs. Hear them whine! How they hated the work and the trail! They were off! Sled after sled churned slowly away into the silence. They were gone. They had passed out of his life, and he faced the last bitter hour alone. No. The snow crunched beneath a moccasin; a man stood beside him; upon his head a hand rested gently. His son was good to do this thing. He remembered other old men whose sons had not waited after the tribe. But his son had. He wandered away into the past, till the young man's voice brought him back.

'Is it well with you?' he asked.

And the old man answered, 'It is well.'

'There be wood beside you,' the younger man continued, 'and the fire burns bright. The morning is grey, and the cold has broken. It will snow presently. Even now is it snowing.'

'Ay, even now is it snowing.'

'The tribesmen hurry. Their bales are heavy, and their bellies flat with lack of feasting. The trail is long and they travel fast. I go now. It is well?'

'It is well. I am as a last year's leaf, clinging lightly to the stem. The first breath that blows, and I fall. My voice is become like an old woman's. My eyes no longer show me the way of my feet, and my feet are heavy, and I am tired. It is well.'

He bowed his head in content till the last noise of the complaining snow had died away, and he knew his son was beyond recall. Then his hand crept out in haste to the wood. It alone stood between him and the eternity that yawned in upon him. At last the measure of his life was a handful of faggots. One by one they would go to feed the fire, and just so, step by step, death would creep upon him. When the last stick had surrendered up its heat, the frost would begin to gather strength. First his feet would yield, then his hands; and the numbness would travel, slowly, from the extremities to the body. His head would fall forward upon his knees, and he would rest. It was easy. All men must die.

He did not complain. It was the way of life, and it was just. He had been born close to the earth, close to the earth had he lived, and the law thereof was not new to him. It was the law of all flesh. Nature was not kindly to the flesh. She had no concern for that concrete thing called the individual. Her interest lay in the species, the race. This was the deepest abstraction old Koskoosh's barbaric mind was capable of, but he grasped it firmly. He saw it exemplified in all life. The rise of the sap, the bursting greenness of the willow bud, the fall of the yellow leaf—in this alone was told the whole history. But one task did Nature set the individual. Did he not perform it, he died. Did he perform it, it was all the same, he died. Nature did not care; there were plenty who were obedient, and it was only the obedience in this matter, not the obedient, which lived and lived always. The tribe of Koskoosh was very old. The old men he had known when a boy, had known old men before them. Therefore it was true that the tribe lived, that it stood for the obedience of all its members, way down into the forgotten past, whose very resting-places were unremembered. They did not count; they were episodes. They had passed away like clouds from a summer sky. He also was an episode, and would pass away. Nature did not care. To life she set one task, gave one law. To perpetuate was the task of life, its law was death. A maiden was a good creature to look upon, full-breasted and strong, with spring to her step and light in her eyes. But her task was yet before her. The light in her eyes brightened, her step quickened, she was now bold with the young men, now timid, and she gave them of her own unrest. And ever she grew fairer and yet fairer to look upon, till some hunter, able no longer to withhold himself, took her to his lodge to cook and toil for him and to become the mother of his children. And with the coming of her offspring her looks left her. Her limbs dragged and shuffled, her eyes dimmed and bleared, and only the little children found joy against the withered cheek of the old squaw by the fire. Her task was done. But a little while, on the first pinch of famine or the first long trail, and she would be left, even as he had been left, in the snow, with a little pile of wood. Such was the law.

He placed a stick carefully upon the fire and resumed his meditations. It was the same everywhere, with all things. The mosquitos vanished with the first frost. The little tree-squirrel crawled away to die. When age settled upon the rabbit it became slow and heavy, and could no longer out-foot its enemies. Even the big bald-face grew clumsy and blind and quarrelsome, in the end to be dragged down by a handful of yelping huskies. He remembered how he had abandoned his own father on an upper reach of the Klondike one winter, the winter before the missionary came with his talk-books and his box of medicines. Many a time had Koskoosh smacked his lips over the recollection of that box, though now his mouth refused to moisten. The 'pain-killer' had been especially good. But the missionary was a bother after all, for he brought no meat into the camp, and he ate heartily, and the hunters grumbled. But he chilled his lungs on the divide by the Mayo, and the dogs afterwards nosed the stones away and fought over his bones.

Koskoosh placed another stick on the fire and harked back deeper into the past. There was the time of the Great Famine, when the old men crouched empty-bellied to the fire, and let fall from their lips dim traditions of the ancient day when the Yukon ran wide open for three winters, and then lay frozen for three summers. He had lost his mother in that famine. In the summer the salmon run had failed, and the tribe looked forward to the winter and the coming of the caribou. Then the winter came, but with it there were no caribou. Never had the like been known, not even in the lives of the old men. But the caribou did not come, and it was the seventh year, and the rabbits had not replenished, and the dogs were naught but bundles of bones. And through the long darkness the children wailed and died, and the women, and the old men; and not

H

one in ten of the tribe lived to meet the sun when it came back in the spring. That was a famine!

But he had seen times of plenty, too, when the meat spoiled on their hands, and the dogs were fat and worthless with over-eating—times when they let the game go unkilled, and the women were fertile, and the lodges were cluttered with sprawling men-children and women-children. Then it was the men became high-stomached, and revived ancient quarrels, and crossed the divides to the south to kill the Pellys, and to the west that they might sit by the dead fires of the Tananas. He remembered, when a boy, during a time of plenty, when he saw a moose pulled down by the wolves. Zing-ha lay with him in the snow and watched—Zing-ha, who later became the craftiest of hunters, and who, in the end, fell through an air-hole on the Yukon. They found him, a month afterwards, just as he had crawled half-way out and frozen stiff to the ice.

But the moose. Zing-ha and he had gone out that day to play at hunting after the manner of their fathers. On the bed of the creek they struck the fresh track of a moose, and with it the tracks of many wolves. 'An old one,' Zing-ha, who was quicker at reading the sign, said, 'an old one who cannot keep up with the herd. The wolves have cut him out from his brothers, and they will never leave him.' And it was so. It was their way. By day and by night, never resting, snarling on his heels, snapping at his nose, they would stay by him to the end. How Zing-ha and he felt the blood-lust quicken! The finish would be a sight to see!

Eager-footed, they took the trail, and even he, Koskoosh, slow of sight and an unversed tracker, could have followed it blind, it was so wide. Hot were they on the heels of the chase, reading the grim tragedy, fresh-written, at every step. Now they came to where the moose had made a stand. Thrice the length of a grown man's body, in every direction, had the snow been stamped about and up-tossed. In the midst were the deep impressions of the splay-hoofed game, and all about, everywhere, were the lighter footmarks of the wolves. Some, while their brothers harried the kill, had lain to one side and rested. The full-stretched impress of their bodies in the snow was as perfect as though made the moment before. One wolf had been caught in a wild lunge of the maddened victim and trampled to death. A few bones, well picked, bore witness.

Again, they ceased the uplift of their snow-shoes at a second stand. Here the great animal had fought desperately. Twice had he been dragged down, as the snow attested, and twice had he shaken his assailants clear and gained footing once more. He had done his task long since, but none the less was life dear to him. Zing-ha said it was a strange thing, a moose once down to get free again, but this one certainly had. The shaman would see signs and wonders in this when they told him.

And yet again, they came to where the moose had made to mount the bank and gain the timber. But his foes had laid on from behind, till he reared and fell back upon them, crushing two deep into the snow. It was plain the kill was at hand, for their brothers had left them untouched. Two more stands were hurried past, brief in time-length and very close together. The trail was red now, and the clean stride of the great beast had grown short and slovenly. Then they heard the first sounds of the battle—not the full-throated chorus of the chase, but the short, snappy bark which spoke of close quarters and teeth to flesh. Crawling up the wind, Zing-ha bellied it through the snow, and with him crept he, Koskoosh, who was to be chief of the tribesmen in the years to come. Together they shoved aside the under branches of a young spruce and peered forth. It was the end they saw.

The picture, like all of youth's impressions, was still strong with him, and his dim eyes watched the end played out as vividly as in that far-off time. Koskoosh marvelled at this, for in the days which followed, when he was a leader of men and a head of councillors, he had done great deeds and made his name a curse in the mouths of the Pellys, to say naught of the strange white man he had killed, knife to knife, in open fight.

For long he pondered on the days of his youth, till the fire died down and the frost bit deeper. He replenished it with two sticks this time, and gauged his grip on life by what remained. If Sit-cum-to-ha had only remembered her grandfather, and gathered a larger armful, his hours would have been longer. It would have been easy. But she was ever a careless child, and honoured not her ancestors from the time the Beaver, son of the son of Zing-ha, first cast eyes upon her. Well, what mattered it? Had he not done likewise in his own quick youth? For a while he listened to the silence. Perhaps the heart of his son might soften, and he would come back with the dogs to take his old father on with the tribe to where the caribou ran thick and the fat hung heavy upon them.

He strained his ears, his restless brain for the moment stilled. Not a stir, nothing. He alone took breath in the midst of the great silence. It was very lonely. Hark! What was that? A chill passed over his body. The familiar, long-drawn howl broke the void, and it was close at hand. Then on his darkened eyes was projected the vision of the moose—the old bull moose—the torn flanks and bloody sides, the riddled mane, and the great branching horns, down low and tossing to the last. He saw the flashing forms of grey, the gleaming eyes, the lolling tongues, the slavered fangs. And he saw the inexorable circle close in till it became a dark point in the midst of the stamped snow.

A cold muzzle thrust against his cheek, and at its touch his soul leaped back to the present. His hand shot into the fire and dragged out a burning faggot. Overcome for the nonce by his hereditary fear of man, the brute retreated, raising a prolonged call to his brothers; and greedily they answered, till a ring of crouching, jaw-slobbered grey was stretched round about. The old man listened to the drawing in of his circle. He waved his brand wildly, and sniffs turned to snarls; but the panting brutes refused to scatter. Now one wormed his chest forward, dragging his haunches after, now a second, now a third; but never a one drew back. Why should he cling to life?

he asked, and dropped the blazing stick into the snow. It sizzled and went out. The circle grunted uneasily, but held its own. Again he saw the last stand of the old bull moose, and Koskoosh dropped his head wearily upon his knees. What did it matter after all? Was it not the law of life?

South of the Slot

OLD San Francisco, which is the San Francisco of only the other day, the day before the earthquake, was divided midway by the Slot. The Slot was an iron crack that ran along the centre of Market Street, and from the Slot arose the burr of the ceaseless, endless cable that was hitched at will to the cars it dragged up and down. In truth, there were two slots, but in the quick grammar of the West time was saved by calling them, and much more that they stood for, 'The Slot'. North of the Slot were the theatres, hotels, and shopping district, the banks and the staid, respectable business houses. South of the Slot were the factories, slums, laundries, machine-shops, boiler works, and the abodes of the working class.

The Slot was the metaphor that expressed the class cleavage of Society, and no man crossed this metaphor, back and forth, more successfully than Freddie Drummond. He made a practice of living in both worlds, and in both worlds he lived signally well. Freddie Drummond was a professor in the Sociology Department of the University of California, and it was as a professor of sociology that he first crossed over the Slot, lived for six months in the great labour-ghetto, and wrote *The Unskilled Labourer*—a book that was hailed everywhere as an able contribution to the literature of progress, and as a splendid reply to the literature of discontent. Politically and economically it was nothing if not orthodox. Presidents of great railway systems bought whole editions of it to give to their employees. The Manufacturers' Association alone distributed fifty thousand copies of it. In a way, it was almost as immoral as the far-famed and notorious *Message to Garcia*, while in its pernicious preachment of thrift and content it ran *Mrs. Wiggs of the Cabbage Patch* a close second.

At first, Freddie Drummond found it monstrously difficult to get along among the working people. He was not used to their ways, and they certainly were not used to his. They were suspicious. He had no antecedents. He could talk of no previous jobs. His hands were soft. His extraordinary politeness was ominous. His first idea of the role he would play was that of a free and independent American who chose to work with his hands and no explanations given. But it wouldn't do, as he quickly discovered. At the beginning they accepted him, very provisionally, as a freak. A little later, as he began to know his way about better, he insensibly drifted into the role that would work—namely, he was a man who had seen better days, but who was down on his luck, though, to be sure, only temporarily.

He learned many things, and generalized much and often erroneously, all of which can be found in the pages of *The Unskilled Labourer*. He saved himself, however, after the sane and conservative manner of his kind, by labelling his generalizations as 'tentative'. One of his first experiences was in the great Wilmax Cannery, where he was put on piece-work making small packing cases. A box factory supplied the parts, and all Freddie Drummond had to do was to fit the parts into a form and drive in the wire nails with a light hammer.

It was not skilled labour, but it was piece-work. The ordinary labourers in the cannery got a dollar and a half per day. Freddie Drummond found the other men on the same job with him jogging along and earning a dollar and seventy-five cents a day. By the third day he was able to earn the same. But he was ambitious. He did not care to jog along and, being unusually able and fit, on the fourth day earned two dollars.

The next day, having keyed himself up to an exhausting high-tension, he earned two dollars and a half. His fellow workers favoured him with scowls and black looks, and made remarks, slangily witty and which he did not understand, about sucking up to the boss and pace-making and holding her down when the rains set in. He was astonished at their malingering on piece-work, generalized about the inherent laziness of the unskilled labourer, and proceeded next day to hammer out three dollars' worth of boxes.

And that night, coming out of the cannery, he was interviewed by his fellow workmen, who were very angry and incoherently slangy. He failed to comprehend the motive behind their action. The action itself was strenuous. When he refused to ease down his pace and bleated about freedom of contract, independent Americanism, and the dignity of toil, they proceeded to spoil his pace-making ability. It was a fierce battle, for Drummond was a large man and an athlete, but the crowd finally jumped on his ribs, walked on his face, and stamped on his fingers, so that it was only after lying in bed for a week that he was able to get up and look for another job. All of which is duly narrated in that first book of his, in the chapter entitled 'The Tyranny of Labour'.

A little later, in another department of the Wilmax Cannery, lumping as a fruit-distributor among the women, he essayed to carry two boxes of fruit at a time, and was promptly reproached by the other fruit-lumpers. It was palpable malingering; but he was there, he decided, not to change conditions, but to observe. So he lumped one box thereafter, and so well did he study the art of shirking that he wrote a special chapter on it, with the last several paragraphs devoted to tentative generalizations.

In those six months he worked at many jobs and developed into a very good imitation of a genuine worker. He was a natural linguist, and he kept notebooks, making a scientific study of the workers' slang or argot, until he could talk quite intelligibly. This language also enabled him more intimately to follow their mental processes, and thereby to gather much data for a projected chapter in some future book which he planned to entitle *Synthesis of Working-Class Psychology*.

Before he arose to the surface from that first plunge into the underworld he discovered that he was a good actor and demonstrated the plasticity of his nature. He was himself astonished at his own fluidity. Once having mastered the language and conquered numerous fastidious qualms, he found that he could flow into any nook of working-class life and fit it so snugly as to feel comfortably at home. As he said, in the preface to his second book, *The Toiler*, he endeavoured really to know the working people, and the only possible way to achieve this was to work beside them, eat their food, sleep in their beds, be amused with their amusements, think their thoughts, and feel their feeling.

He was not a deep thinker. He had no faith in new theories. All his norms and criteria were conventional. His Thesis on the French Revolution was noteworthy in college annals, not merely for its painstaking and voluminous accuracy, but for the fact that it was the dryest, deadest, most formal, and most orthodox screed ever written on the subject. He was a very reserved man, and his natural inhibition was large in quantity and steel-like in quality. He had but few friends. He was too undemonstrative, too frigid. He had no vices, nor had any one ever discovered any temptations. Tobacco he detested, beer he abhorred, and he was never known to drink anything stronger than an occasional light wine at dinner.

When a freshman he had been baptized 'Ice-Box' by his warmer-blooded fellows. As a member of the faculty he was known as 'Cold-Storage'. He had but one grief, and that was 'Freddie'. He had earned it when he played full-back in the 'Varsity eleven, and his formal soul had never succeeded in living it down. 'Freddie' he would ever be, except officially, and through nightmare vistas he looked into a future when his world would speak of him as 'Old Freddie'.

For he was very young to be a doctor of sociology, only twenty-seven, and he looked younger. In appearance and atmosphere he was a strapping big college man, smooth-faced and easy-mannered, clean and simple and wholesome, with a known record of being a splendid athlete and an implied vast possession of cold culture of the inhibited sort. He never talked shop out of class and committee rooms, except later on, when his books showered him with distasteful public notice and he yielded to the extent of reading occasional papers before certain literary and economic societies.

He did everything right—too right; and in dress and comportment was inevitably correct. Not that he was a dandy. Far from it. He was a college man, in dress and carriage as like as a pea to the type that of late years is being so generously turned out of our institutions of higher learning. His handshake was satisfyingly strong and stiff. His blue eyes were coldly blue and convincingly sincere. His voice, firm and masculine, clean and crisp of enunciation, was pleasant to the ear. The one drawback to Freddie Drummond was his inhibition. He never unbent. In his football days, the higher the tension of the game, the cooler he grew. He was noted as a boxer, but he was regarded as an automaton, with the inhuman precisions of a machine judging distance and timing blows, guarding, blocking, and stalling. He was rarely punished himself, while he rarely punished an opponent. He was too clever and too controlled to permit himself to put a pound more weight into a punch than he intended. With him it was a matter of exercise. It kept him fit.

As time went by, Freddie Drummond found himself more frequently crossing the Slot and losing himself in South of Market. His summer and winter holidays were spent there, and, whether it was a week or a week-end, he found the time spent there to be valuable and enjoyable. And there was so much material to be gathered. His third book, *Mass and Master*, became a textbook in the American universities; and almost before he knew it, he was at work on a fourth one, *The Fallacy of the Inefficient*.

Somewhere in his make-up there was a strange twist or quirk. Perhaps it was a recoil from his environment and training, or from the tempered seed of his ancestors, who had been bookmen generation preceding generation; but at any rate, he found enjoyment in being down in the working-class world. In his own world he was 'Cold Storage', but down below he was 'Big' Bill Totts, who could drink and smoke, and slang and fight, and be an all-round favourite. Everybody liked Bill, and more than one working girl made love to him. At first he had been merely a good actor, but as time went on, simulation became second nature. He no longer played a part, and he loved sausages, sausages and bacon, than which, in his own proper sphere, there was nothing more loathsome in the way of food.

From doing the thing for the need's sake, he came to doing

the thing for the thing's sake. He found himself regretting as the time drew near for him to go back to his lecture-room and his inhibition. And he often found himself waiting with anticipation for the dreamy time to pass when he could cross the Slot and cut loose and play the devil. He was not wicked, but as 'Big' Bill Totts he did a myriad things that Freddie Drummond would never have been permitted to do. Moreover, Freddie Drummond never would have wanted to do them. That was the strangest part of his discovery. Freddie Drummond and Bill Totts were two totally different creatures. The desires and tastes and impulses of each ran counter to the other's. Bill Totts could shirk at a job with clear conscience, while Freddie Drummond condemned shirking as vicious, criminal, and un-American, and devoted whole chapters to condemnation of the vice. Freddie Drummond did not care for dancing, but Bill Totts never missed the nights at the various dancing clubs, such as The Magnolia, The Western Star, and The Elite; while he won a massive silver cup, standing thirty inches high, for being the best-sustained character at the Butchers' and Meat Workers' annual grand masked ball. And Bill Totts liked the girls and the girls liked him, while Freddie Drummond enjoyed playing the ascetic in this particular, was open in his opposition to equal suffrage, and cynically bitter in his secret condemnation of co-education.

Freddie Drummond changed his manners with his dress, and without effort. When he entered the obscure little room used for his transformation scenes, he carried himself just a bit too stiffly. He was too erect, his shoulders were an inch too far back, while his face was grave, almost harsh, and practically expressionless. But when he emerged in Bill Totts' clothes he was another creature. Bill Totts did not slouch, but somehow his whole form limbered up and became graceful. The very sound of the voice was changed, and the laugh was loud and hearty, while loose speech and an occasional oath were as a matter of course on his lips. Also, Bill Totts was a trifle inclined to late hours, and at times, in saloons, to be good-naturedly bellicose with other workmen. Then, too, at Sunday picnics or when coming home from the show, either arm betrayed a practised familiarity in stealing around girls' waists, while he displayed a wit keen and delightful in the flirtatious badinage that was expected of a good fellow in his class.

So thoroughly was Bill Totts himself, so thoroughly a workman, a genuine denizen of South of the Slot, that he was as class-conscious as the average of his kind, and his hatred for a scab even exceeded that of the average loyal union man. During the Water Front Strike, Freddie Drummond was somehow able to stand apart from the unique combination, and, coldly critical, watch Bill Totts hilariously slug scab longshoremen. For Bill Totts was a dues-paying member of the Longshoremen's Union and had a right to be indignant with the usurpers of his job. 'Big' Bill Totts was so very big, and so very able, that it was 'Big' Bill to the front when trouble was brewing. From acting outraged feelings, Freddie Drummond, in the role of his other self, came to experience genuine outrage, and it was only when he returned to the classic atmosphere of the university that he was able, sanely and conservatively, to generalize upon his underworld experiences and put them down on paper as a trained sociologist should. That Bill Totts lacked the perspective to raise him above class-consciousness Freddie Drummond clearly saw. But Bill Totts could not see it. When he saw a scab taking his job away, he saw red at the same time, and little else did he see. It was Freddie Drummond, irreproachably clothed and comported, seated at his study desk or facing his class in *Sociology* 17, who saw Bill Totts, and all around Bill Totts, and all around the whole scab and union-labour problem and its relation to world market. Bill Totts really wasn't able to see beyond the the economic welfare of the United States in the struggle for the next meal and the prize-fight the following night at the Gaiety Athletic Club.

It was while gathering material for *Women and Work* that Freddie received his first warning of the danger he was in. He was too successful at living in both worlds. This strange dualism he had developed was after all very unstable, and, as he sat in his study and meditated, he saw that it could not endure. It was really a transition stage, and if he persisted he saw that he would inevitably have to drop one world or the other. He could not continue in both. And as he looked at the row of volumes that graced the upper shelf of his revolving bookcase, his volumes, beginning with his Thesis and ending with *Women and Work*, he decided that that was the world he would hold to and stick by. Bill Totts had served his purpose, but he had become a too dangerous accomplice. Bill Totts would have to cease.

Freddie Drummond's fright was due to Mary Condon, President of the International Glove Workers' Union No. 974. He had seen her, first, from the spectators' galley, at the annual convention of the Northwest Federation of Labour, and he had seen her through Bill Totts' eyes, and that individual had been most favourably impressed by her. She was not Freddie Drummond's sort at all. What if she were a royal-bodied woman, graceful and sinewy as a panther, with amazing black eyes that could fill with fire or laughter-love, as the mood might dictate? He detested women with a too exuberant vitality and a lack of . . . well, of inhibition. Freddie Drummond accepted the doctrine of evolution because it was quite universally accepted by college men, and he flatly believed that man had climbed up the ladder of life out of the weltering muck and mess of lower and monstrous organic things. But he was a trifle ashamed of this genealogy, and preferred not to think of it. Wherefore, probably, he practised his iron inhibition and preached it to others, and preferred women of his own type, who could shake free of this bestial and regrettable ancestral line and by discipline and control emphasize the wideness of the gulf that separated them from what their dim forebears had been.

Bill Totts had none of these considerations, He had liked Mary Condon from the moment his eyes first rested on her in the convention hall, and he had made it a point, then and there, to find out who she was. The next time he met her, and quite by accident, was when he was driving an express wagon for Pat Morrissey. It was in a lodging-house in Mission Street, where he had been called to take a trunk into storage. The landlady's daughter had called him and led him to the little bedroom, the occupant of which, a glove-maker, had just been removed to hospital. But Bill did not know this. He stooped, up-ended the trunk, which was a large one, got it on his shoulder, and struggled with his back towards the open door. At that moment he heard a woman's voice.

'Belong to the union?' was the question asked.

'Aw, what's it to you?' he retorted. 'Run along now, an' git outa my way. I wanta turn round.'

The next he knew, big as he was, he was whirled half around and sent reeling backward, the trunk overbalancing him, till he fetched up with a crash against the wall. He started to swear, but at the same instant found himself looking into Mary Condon's flashing, angry eyes.

'Of course I b'long to the union,' he said. 'I was only kiddin' you.'

'Where's your card?' she demanded in business-like tones.

'In my pocket. But I can't git it now. This trunk's too damn heavy. Come on down to the wagon an' I'll show it to you.'

'Put that trunk down,' was the command.

'What for? I got a card, I'm tellin' you.'

'Put it down, that's all. No scab's going to handle that trunk. You ought to be ashamed of yourself, you big coward, scabbing on honest men. Why don't you join the union and be a man?'

Mary Condon's colour had left her face, and it was apparent that she was in a rage.

'To think of a big man like you turning traitor to his class. I suppose you're aching to join the militia for a chance to shoot down union drivers the next strike. You may belong to the militia already, for that matter. You're the sort——'

'Hold on, now, that's too much!' Bill dropped the trunk to the floor with a bang, straightened up, and thrust his hand into his inside coat pocket. 'I told you I was only kiddin'. There, look at that.'

It was a union card properly enough.

'All right, take it along,' Mary Condon said. 'And the next time don't kid.'

Her face relaxed as she noticed the ease with which he got the big trunk to his shoulder, and her eyes glowed as they glanced over the graceful massiveness of the man. But Bill did not see that. He was too busy with the trunk.

The next time he saw Mary Condon was during the Laundry Strike. The Laundry Workers, but recently organized, were green at the business, and had petitioned Mary Condon to engineer the strike. Freddie Drummond had had an inkling of what was coming, and had sent Bill Totts to join the union and investigate. Bill's job was in the wash-room, and the men had been called out first, that morning, in order to stiffen the courage of the girls; and Bill chanced to be near the door to the mangle-room when Mary Condon started to enter. The superintendent, who was both large and stout, barred her way. He wasn't going to have his girls called out, and he'd teach her a lesson to mind her own business. And as Mary tried to squeeze past him he thrust her back with a rat hand on her shoulder. She glanced around and saw Bill.

'Here you, Mr. Totts,' she called. 'Lend a hand. I want to get in.'

Bill experienced a startle of warm surprise. She had remembered his name from his union card. The next moment the superintendent had been plucked from the doorway raving about rights under the law, and the girls were deserting their machines. During the rest of that short and successful strike, Bill constituted himself Mary Condon's henchman and messenger, and when it was over returned to the University to be Freddie Drummond and to wonder what Bill Totts could see in such a woman.

Freddie Drummond was entirely safe, but Bill had fallen in love. There was no getting away from the fact of it, and it was this fact that had given Freddie Drummond his warning. Well, he had done his work, and his adventures would cease. There was no need for him to cross the Slot again. All but the last three chapters of his latest, *Labour Tactics and Strategy*, was finished, and he had sufficient material on hand adequately to supply those chapters.

Another conclusion he arrived at, was that in order to sheet-anchor himself as Freddie Drummond, closer ties and relations in his own social nook were necessary. It was time that he was married, anyway, and he was fully aware that if Freddie Drummond didn't get married, Bill Totts assuredly would, and the complications were too awful to contemplate. And so, enters Catherine Van Vorst. She was a college woman herself, and her father, the one wealthy member of the faculty, was the head of the Philosophy Department as well. It would be a wise marriage from every standpoint, Freddie Drummond concluded when the engagement was consummated and announced. In appearance cold and reserved, aristocratic and wholesomely conservative, Catherine Van Vorst, though warm in her way, possessed an inhibition equal to Drummond's.

All seemed well with him, but Freddie Drummond could not quite shake off the call of the underworld, the lure of the free and open, of the unhampered, irresponsible life south of the Slot. As the time of his marriage approached, he felt that he had indeed sowed wild oats, and he felt, moreover, what a good thing it would be if he could have but one wild fling more, play the good fellow and the wastrel one last time, ere he settled down to grey lecture-rooms and sober matrimony. And, further to tempt him, the very last chapter of *Labour Tactics and Strategy* remained unwritten for lack of a trifle more of essential data which he had neglected to gather.

So Freddie Drummond went down for the last time as Bill Totts, got his data, and, unfortunately, encountered Mary Condon. Once more installed in his study, it was not a pleasant thing to look back upon. It made his warning doubly imperative. Bill Totts had behaved abominably. Not only had he met Mary Condon at the Central Labour Council, but he had stopped at a chop-house with her, on the way home, and treated her to oysters. And before they parted at her door, his arms had been about her, and he had kissed her on the lips and kissed her repeatedly. And her last words in his ear, words

uttered softly with a catchy sob in the throat that was nothing
more nor less than a love cry, were 'Bill . . . dear, dear Bill'.

Freddie Drummond shuddered at the recollection. He saw
the pit yawning for him. He was not by nature a polygamist,
and he was appalled at the possibilities of the situation. It
would have to be put an end to, and it would end in one only
of two ways: either he must become wholly Bill Totts and be
married to Mary Condon, or he must remain wholly Freddie
Drummond and be married to Catherine Van Vorst. Otherwise, his conduct would be beneath contempt and horrible.

In the several months that followed, San Francisco was torn
with labour strife. The unions and the employers' associations
had locked horns with a determination that looked as if they
intended to settle the matter, one way or the other, for all time.
But Freddie Drummond corrected proofs, lectured classes, and
did not budge. He devoted himself to Catherine Van Vorst,
and day by day found more to respect and admire in her—nay,
even to love in her. The Street Car Strike tempted him, but
not so severely as he would have expected; and the great Meat
Strike came on and left him cold. The ghost of Bill Totts had
been successfully laid, and Freddie Drummond with rejuvenes-
cent zeal tackled a brochure, long-planned, on the topic of
'diminishing returns'.

The wedding was two weeks off, when, one afternoon, in
San Francisco, Catherine Van Vorst picked him up and whisked
him away to see a Boys' Club, recently instituted by the settlement workers in whom she was interested. It was her brother's
machine, but they were alone with the exception of the chauffeur. At the junction with Kearney Street, Market and Geary
Streets intersect like the sides of a sharp-angled letter 'V'.
They, in the auto, were coming down Market with the intention of negotiating the sharp apex and going up Geary. But
they did not know what was coming down Geary, timed by
fate to meet them at the apex. While aware from the papers
that the Meat Strike was on and that it was an exceedingly
bitter one, all thought of it at that moment was farthest
from Freddie Drummond's mind. Was he not seated beside

Catherine? And besides, he was carefully expositing to her his views on settlement work—views that Bill Totts' adventures had played a part in formulating.

Coming down Geary Street were six meat wagons. Beside each scab driver sat a policeman. Front and rear, and along each side of this procession, marched a protecting escort of one hundred police. Behind the police rearguard, at a respectful distance, was an orderly but vociferous mob, several blocks in length, that congested the street from sidewalk to sidewalk. The Beef Trust was making an effort to supply the hotels, and, incidentally, to begin the breaking of the strike. The St. Francis had already been supplied, at a cost of many broken windows and broken heads, and the expedition was marching to the relief of the Palace Hotel.

All unwitting, Drummond sat beside Catherine, talking settlement work, as the auto, honking methodically and dodging traffic, swung in a wide curve to get round the apex. A big coal wagon, loaded with lump coal and drawn by four huge horses, just debouching from Kearney Street as though to turn down Market, blocked their way. The driver of the wagon seemed undecided, and the chauffeur, running slow but disregarding some shouted warning from the crossing policemen, swerved the auto to the left, violating the traffic rules, in order to pass in front of the wagon.

At that moment Freddie Drummond discontinued his conversation. Nor did he resume it again, for the situation was developing with the rapidity of a transformation scene. He heard the roar of the mob at the rear, and caught a glimpse of the helmeted police and the lurching meat wagons. At the same moment, laying on his whip and standing up to his task, the coal driver rushed horses and wagon squarely in front of the advancing procession, pulled the horses up sharply, and put on the big brake. Then he made his lines fast to the brake-handle and sat down with the air of one who had stopped to stay. The auto had been brought to a stop, too, by his big panting leaders which had jammed against it.

Before the chauffeur could back clear, an old Irishman,

driving a rickety express wagon and lashing his one horse to a gallop, had locked wheels with the auto. Drummond recognized both horse and wagon, for he had driven them often himself. The Irishman was Pat Morrissey. On the other side a brewery wagon was locking with the coal wagon, and an eastbound Kearney Street car, wildly clanging its gong, the motorman shouting defiance at the crossing policeman, was dashing forward to complete the blockade. And wagon after wagon was locking and blocking and adding to the confusion. The meat wagons halted. The police were trapped. The roar at the rear increased as the mob came on to the attack, while the vanguard of the police charged the obstructing wagons.

'We're in for it,' Drummond remarked coolly to Catherine.

'Yes,' she nodded, with equal coolness. 'What savages they are.'

His admiration for her doubled on itself. She was indeed his sort. He would have been satisfied with her even if she had screamed and clung to him, but this—this was magnificent. She sat in that storm centre as calmly as if it had been no more than a block of carriages at the opera.

The police were struggling to clear a passage. The driver of the coal wagon, a big man in shirt sleeves, lighted a pipe and sat smoking. He glanced down complacently at a captain of police who was raving and cursing at him, and his only acknowledgement was a shrug of the shoulders. From the rear arose the rat-tat-tat of clubs on heads and a pandemonium of cursing, yelling, and shouting. A violent accession of noise proclaimed that the mob had broken through and was dragging a scab from a wagon. The police captain reinforced from his vanguard, and the mob at the rear was repelled. Meanwhile, window after window in the high office building on the right had been opened, and the class-conscious clerks were raining a shower of office furniture down on the heads of police and scabs. Waste-baskets, ink-bottles, paper-weights, typewriters—anything and everything that came to hand was filling the air.

A policeman, under orders from his captain, clambered to

the lofty seat of the coal wagon to arrest the driver. And the driver, rising leisurely and peacefully to meet him, suddenly crumpled him in his arms and threw him down on top of the captain. The driver was a young giant, and when he climbed on his load and poised a lump of coal in both hands, a policeman, who was just scaling the wagon from the side, let go and dropped back to earth. The captain ordered half a dozen of his men to take the wagon. The teamster, scrambling over the load from side to side, beat them down with huge lumps of coal.

The crowd on the sidewalks and the teamsters on the locked wagons roared encouragement and their own delight. The motorman, smashing helmets with his controller bar, was beaten into insensibility and dragged from his platform. The captain of police, beside himself at the repulse of his men, led the next assault on the coal wagon. A score of police were swarming up the tall-sided fortress. But the teamster multiplied himself. At times there were six or eight policemen rolling on the pavement and under the wagon. Engaged in repulsing an attack on the rear end of his fortress, the teamster turned about to see the captain just in the act of stepping on to the seat from the front end. He was still in the air and in most unstable equilibrium, when the teamster hurled a thirty-pound lump of coal. It caught the captain fairly on the chest, and he went over backward, striking on a wheeler's back, tumbling on to the ground, and jamming against the rear wheel of the auto.

Catherine thought he was dead, but he picked himself up and charged back. She reached out her gloved hand and patted the flank of the snorting, quivering horse. But Drummond did not notice the action. He had eyes for nothing save the battle of the coal wagon, while somewhere in his complicated psychology, one Bill Totts was heaving and straining in an effort to come to life. Drummond believed in law and order and the maintenance of the established, but this riotous savage within him would have none of it. Then, if ever, did Freddie Drummond call upon his iron inhibition to save him. But it is written that the house divided against itself must fall. And Freddie

Drummond found that he had divided all the will and the force of him with Bill Totts, and between them the entity that constituted the pair of them was being wrenched in twain.

Freddie Drummond sat in the auto, quite composed, alongside Catherine Van Vorst; but looking out of Freddie Drummond's eyes was Bill Totts, and somewhere behind those eyes, battling for the control of their mutual body, were Freddie Drummond, the sane and conservative sociologist, and Bill Totts, the class-conscious and bellicose union working man. It was Bill Totts, looking out of those eyes, who saw the inevitable end of the battle on the coal wagon. He saw a policeman gain the top of the load, a second, and a third. They lurched clumsily on the loose footing, but their long riot-clubs were out and swinging. One blow caught the teamster on the head. A second he dodged, receiving it on the shoulder. For him the game was plainly up. He dashed in suddenly, clutched two policemen in his arms, and hurled himself a prisoner to the pavement, his hold never relaxing on his two captors.

Catherine Van Vorst was sick and faint at the sight of the blood and brutal fighting. But her qualms were vanquished by the sensational and most unexpected happening that followed. The man beside her emitted an unearthly and uncultured yell and rose to his feet. She saw him spring over the front seat, leap to the broad rump of the wheeler, and from there gain the wagon. His onslaught was like a whirlwind. Before the bewildered officer on the load could guess the errand of this conventionally clad but excited-seeming gentleman, he was the recipient of a punch that arched him back through the air to the pavement. A kick in the face led an ascending policeman to follow his example. A rush of three more gained the top and locked with Bill Totts in a gigantic clinch, during which his scalp was opened up by a club, and coat, vest, and half his starched shirt were torn from him. But the three policemen were flung far and wide, and Bill Totts, raining down lumps of coal, held the fort.

The captain led gallantly to the attack, but was bowled over by a chunk of coal that burst on his head in black baptism. The need of the police was to break the blockade in front before the mob could break in at the rear, and Bill Totts' need was to hold the wagon till the mob did break through. So the battle of the coal went on.

The crowd had recognized its champion. 'Big' Bill, as usual, had come to the front, and Catherine Van Vorst was bewildered by the cries of 'Bill! Oh you Bill!' that arose on every hand. Pat Morrissey, on his wagon seat, was jumping and screaming in an ecstasy. 'Eat 'em, Bill! Eat 'em! Eat 'em alive!' From the sidewalk she heard a woman's voice cry out, 'Look out, Bill—front end!' Bill took the warning and with well-directed coal cleared the front end of the wagon of assailants. Catherine Van Vorst turned her head and saw on the kerb of the sidewalk a woman with vivid colouring and flashing black eyes who was staring with all her soul at the man who had been Freddie Drummond a few minutes before.

The windows of the office building became vociferous with applause. A fresh shower of office chairs and filing cabinets descended. The mob had broken through on one side the line of wagons, and was advancing, each segregated policeman the centre of a fighting group. The scabs were torn from their seats, the traces of the horses cut, and the frightened animals put in flight. Many policemen crawled under the coal wagon for safety, while the loose horses, with here and there a policeman on their backs or struggling at their heads to hold them, surged across the sidewalk opposite the jam and broke into Market Street.

Catherine Van Vorst heard the woman's voice calling in warning. She was back on the kerb again, and crying out— 'Beat it, Bill! Now's your time! Beat it!'

The police for the moment had been swept away. Bill Totts leaped to the pavement and made his way to the woman on the sidewalk. Catherine Van Vorst saw her throw her arms around him and kiss him on the lips; and Catherine Van Vorst watched him curiously as he went on down the sidewalk, one arm around the woman. both talking and laughing, and he with a volubility and abandon she could never have dreamed possible.

The police were back again and clearing the jam while waiting for reinforcements and new drivers and horses. The mob had done its work and was scattering, and Catherine Van Vorst, still watching, could see the man she had known as Freddie Drummond. He towered a head above the crowd. His arm was still about the woman. And she in the motor-car, watching, saw the pair cross Market Street, cross the Slot, and disappear down Third Street into the labour ghetto.

.   .   .   .   .

In the years that followed no more lectures were given in the University of California by one Freddie Drummond, and no more books on economics and the labour question appeared over the name of Frederick A. Drummond. On the other hand there arose a new labour leader, William Totts by name. He it was who married Mary Condon, President of the International Glove Workers' Union No. 974; and he it was who called the notorious Cooks' and Waiters' Strike, which, before its successful termination, brought out with it scores of other unions, among which, of the more remotely allied, were the Chicken Pickers and the Undertakers.

The Dream of Debs

I AWOKE fully an hour before my customary time. This in itself was remarkable, and I lay very wide awake, pondering over it. Something was the matter, something was wrong—I knew not what. I was oppressed by a premonition of something terrible that had happened or was about to happen. But what was it? I strove to orient myself. I remembered that at the time of the Great Earthquake of 1906 many claimed that they awakened some moments before the first shock and that during these moments they experienced strange feelings of dread. Was San Francisco again to be visited by earthquake?

I lay there for a full minute, numbly expectant, but there occurred no reeling of walls nor shock and grind of falling masonry. All was quiet. That was it! The silence! No wonder I had been perturbed. The hum of the great live city was strangely absent. The surface cars passed along my street, at that time of day, on an average of one every three minutes; but in the ten succeeding minutes not a car passed. Perhaps it was a street-railway strike, was my thought; or perhaps there had been an accident and the power was shut off. But no, the silence was too profound. I heard no jar and rattle of wagon wheels, nor stamp of iron-shod hoofs straining up the steep cobble-stones.

Pressing the push-button beside my bed, I strove to hear the sound of the bell, though I well knew it was impossible for the sound to rise three storeys to me even if the bell did ring. It rang all right, for a few minutes later Brown entered with the tray and morning paper. Though his features were impassive as ever, I noted a startled, apprehensive light in his eyes. I noted, also, that there was no cream on the tray.

'The creamery did not deliver this morning,' he explained; 'nor did the bakery.'

I glanced again at the tray. There were no fresh French rolls—only slices of stale graham bread from yesterday, the most detestable of bread so far as I was concerned.

'Nothing was delivered this morning, sir,' Brown started to explain apologetically; but I interrupted him.

'The paper?'

'Yes, sir, it was delivered, but it was the only thing, and it is the last time, too. There won't be any paper tomorrow. The paper says so. Can I send out and get you some condensed milk?'

I shook my head, accepted the coffee black, and spread open the paper. The headlines explained everything—explained too much, in fact, for the lengths of pessimism to which the journal went were ridiculous. A general strike, it said, had been called all over the United States; and most foreboding anxieties were expressed concerning the provisioning of the great cities.

I read on hastily, skimming much and remembering much of labour troubles in the past. For a generation the general strike had been the dream of organized labour, which dream had arisen originally in the mind of Debs, one of the great labour leaders of thirty years before. I recollected that in my young college-settlement days I had even written an article on the subject for one of the magazines and that I had entitled it 'The Dream of Debs'. And I must confess that I had treated the idea very cavalierly and academically as a dream and nothing more. Time and the world had rolled on, Gompers was gone, the American Federation of Labour was gone, and gone was Debs with all his wild revolutionary ideas; but the dream had persisted, and here it was at last realized in fact. But I laughed, as I read, at the journal's gloomy outlook. I knew better. I had seen organized labour worsted in too many conflicts. It would be a matter only of days when the thing would be settled. This was a national strike, and it wouldn't take the Government long to break it.

I threw the paper down and proceeded to dress. It would certainly be interesting to be out in the streets of San Francisco when not a wheel was turning and the whole city was taking an enforced vacation.

'I beg your pardon, sir,' Brown said, as he handed me my

cigar-case, 'but Mr. Harmmed has asked to see you before you
go out.'

'Send him in right away,' I answered.

Harmmed was the butler. When he entered I could see he
was labouring under controlled excitement. He came at once
to the point.

'What shall I do, sir? There will be needed provisions, and
the delivery drivers are on strike. And the electricity is shut
off—I guess they're on strike, too.'

'Are the shops open?' I asked.

'Only the small ones, sir. The retail clerks are out, and the
big ones can't open; but the owners and their families are
running the little ones themselves.'

'Then take the machine,' I said, 'and go the rounds and
make your purchases. Buy plenty of everything you need or
may need. Get a box of candles—no, get half a dozen boxes.
And, when you're done, tell Harrison to bring the machine
around to the club for me—not later than eleven.'

Harmmed shook his head gravely. 'Mr. Harrison has struck
along with the Chauffeurs' Union, and I don't know how to
run the machine myself.'

'Oh, ho, he has, has he?' I said. 'Well, when next *Mister*
Harrison happens around you tell him that he can look elsewhere for a position.'

'Yes, sir.'

'You don't happen to belong to a Butlers' Union, do you,
Harmmed?'

'No, sir,' was the answer. 'And even if I did I'd not desert
my employer in a crisis like this. No, sir, I would——'

'All right, thank you,' I said. 'Now you get ready to ac-
company me. I'll run the machine myself, and we'll lay in a
stock of provisions to stand a siege.'

It was a beautiful first of May, even as May days go. The
sky was cloudless, there was no wind, and the air was warm—
almost balmy. Many autos were out, but the owners were
driving them themselves. The streets were crowded but quiet.
The working class, dressed in its Sunday best, was out taking

the air and observing the effects of the strike. It was all so unusual, and withal so peaceful, that I found myself enjoying it. My nerves were tingling with mild excitement. It was a sort of placid adventure. I passed Miss Chickering. She was at the helm of her little runabout. She swung around and came after me, catching me at the corner.

'Oh, Mr. Corf!' she hailed. 'Do you know where I can buy candles? I've been to a dozen shops, and they're all sold out. It's dreadfully awful, isn't it?'

But her sparkling eyes gave the lie to her words. Like the rest of us, she was enjoying it hugely. Quite an adventure it was, getting those candles. It was not until we went across the city and down into the working-class quarter south of Market Street that we found small corner groceries that had not yet sold out. Miss Chickering thought one box was sufficient, but I persuaded her into taking four. My car was large, and I laid in a dozen boxes. There was no telling what delays might arise in the settlement of the strike. Also, I filled the car with sacks of flour, baking-powder, tinned goods, and all the ordinary necessaries of life suggested by Harmmed, who fussed around and clucked over the purchases like an anxious old hen.

The remarkable thing, that first day of the strike, was that no one really apprehended anything serious. The announcement of organized labour in the morning papers that it was prepared to stay out a month or three months was laughed at. And yet that very first day we might have guessed as much from the fact that the working class took practically no part in the great rush to buy provisions. Of course not. For weeks and months, craftily and secretly, the whole working class had been laying in private stocks of provisions. That was why we were permitted to go down and buy out the little groceries in the the working-class neighbourhoods.

It was not until I arrived at the club that afternoon that I began to feel the first alarm. Everything was in confusion. There were no olives for the cocktails, and the service was by hitches and jerks. Most of the men were angry, and all were worried. A babel of voices greeted me as I entered. General

Folsom, nursing his capacious paunch in a window-seat in the smoking-room, was defending himself against half a dozen excited gentlemen who were demanding that he should do something.

'What can I do more than I have done?' he was saying 'There are no orders from Washington. If you gentlemen will get a wire through I'll do anything I am commanded to do. But I don't see what can be done. The first thing I did this morning, as soon as I learned of the strike, was to order in the troops from the Presidio—three thousand of them. They're guarding the banks, the Mint, the post office, and all the public buildings. There is no disorder whatever. The strikers are keeping the peace perfectly. You can't expect me to shoot them down as they walk along the streets with wives and children all in their best bib and tucker.'

'I'd like to know what's happening on Wall Street,' I heard Jimmy Wombold say as I passed along. I could imagine his anxiety, for I knew that he was deep in the big Consolidated-Western deal.

'Say, Corf,' Atkinson bustled up to me, 'is your machine running?'

'Yes,' I answered, 'but what's the matter with your own?'

'Broken down, and the garages are all closed. And my wife's somewhere around Truckee, I think, stalled on the overland. Can't get a wire to her for love or money. She should have arrived this evening. She may be starving. Lend me your machine.'

'Can't get it across the bay,' Halstead spoke up. 'The ferries aren't running. But I tell you what you can do. There's Rollinson—oh, Rollinson, come here a moment. Atkinson wants to get a machine across the bay. His wife is stuck on the overland at Truckee. Can't you bring the *Lurlette* across from Tiburon and carry the machine over for him?'

The *Lurlette* was a two-hundred-ton, ocean-going schooner-yacht.

Rollinson shook his head. 'You couldn't get a longshore-man to land the machine on board, even if I could get the

Lurlette over, which I can't, for the crew are members of the Coast Seamen's union, and they're on strike along with the rest.'

'But my wife may be starving,' I could hear Atkinson wailing as I moved on.

At the other end of the smoking-room I ran into a group of men bunched excitedly and angrily around Bertie Messener. And Bertie was stirring them up and prodding them in his cool, cynical way. Bertie didn't care about the strike. He didn't care much about anything. He was blasé—at least in all the clean things of life; the nasty things had no attraction for him. He was worth twenty millions, all of it in safe investments, and he had never done a tap of productive work in his life—inherited it all from his father and two uncles. He had been everywhere, seen everything, and done everything except get married, and this last in the face of the grim and determined attack of a few hundred ambitious mammas. For years he had been the greatest catch, and as yet he had avoided being caught. He was disgracefully eligible. On top of his wealth he was young, handsome, and, as I said before, clean. He was a great athlete, a young blond god that did everything perfectly and admirably with the solitary exception of matrimony. And he didn't care about anything, had no ambitions, no passions, no desire to do the very things he did so much better than other men.

'This is sedition!' one man in the group was crying. Another called it revolt and revolution, and another called it anarchy.

'I can't see it,' Bertie said. 'I have been out in the streets all morning. Perfect order reigns. I never saw a more law-abiding populace. There's no use calling it names. It's not any of those things. It's just what it claims to be, a general strike, and it's your turn to play, gentlemen.'

'And we'll play all right!' cried Garfield, one of the traction millionaires. 'We'll show this dirt where its place is—the beasts! Wait till the Government takes a hand.'

'But where is the Government?' Bertie interposed. 'It might as well be at the bottom of the sea so far as you're concerned.

You don't know what's happening at Washington. You don't know whether you've got a Government or not.'

'Don't you worry about that,' Garfield blurted out.

'I assure you I'm not worrying,' Bertie smiled languidly. 'But it seems to me it's what you fellows are doing. Look in the glass, Garfield.'

Garfield did not look, but had he looked he would have seen a very excited gentleman with rumpled, iron-grey hair, a flushed face, mouth sullen and vindictive, and eyes wildly gleaming.

'It's not right, I tell you,' little Hanover said; and from his tone I was sure that he had already said it a number of times.

'Now that's going too far, Hanover,' Bertie replied. 'You fellows make me tired. You're all open-shop men. You've eroded my eardrums with your endless gabble for the open shop and the right of a man to work. You've harangued along those lines for years. Labour is doing nothing wrong in going out on this general strike. It is violating no law of God nor man. Don't you talk, Hanover. You've been ringing the changes too long on the God-given right to work . . . or not to work; you can't escape the corollary. It's a dirty little sordid scrap, that's all the whole thing is. You've got labour down and gouged it, and now labour's got you down and is gouging you, that's all, and you're squealing.'

Every man in the group broke out in indignant denials that labour had ever been gouged.

'No, sir!' Garfield was shouting. 'We've done the best for labour. Instead of gouging it, we've given it a chance to live. We've made work for it. Where would labour be if it hadn't been for us?'

'A whole lot better off,' Bertie sneered. 'You've got labour down and gouged it every time you got a chance, and you went out of your way to make chances.'

'No! No!' were the cries.

'There was the teamsters' strike, right here in San Francisco,' Bertie went on imperturbably. 'The Employers' Association precipitated that strike. You know that. And you know I know it, too, for I've sat in these very rooms and heard the inside talk and news of the fight. First you precipitated the strike, then you bought the Mayor and the Chief of Police and broke the strike. A pretty spectacle, you philanthropists getting the teamsters down and gouging them.

'Hold on, I'm not through with you. It's only last year that the labour ticket of Colorado elected a governor. He was never seated. You know why. You know how your brother philanthropists and capitalists of Colorado worked it. It was a case of getting labour down and gouging it. You kept the president of the South-western Amalgamated Association of Miners in jail for three years on trumped-up murder charges, and with him out of the way you broke up the association. That was gouging labour, you'll admit. The third time the graduated income tax was declared unconstitutional was a gouge. So was the eight-hour Bill you killed in the last Congress.

'And of all unmitigated immoral gouges, your destruction of the closed-shop principle was the limit. You know how it was done. You bought out Farburg, the last president of the old American Federation of Labour. He was your creature—or the creature of all the trusts and employers' associations, which is the same thing. You precipitated the big closed-shop strike. Farburg betrayed that strike. You won, and the old American Federation of Labour crumbled to pieces. You fellows destroyed it, and by so doing undid yourselves; for right on top of it began the organization of the I.L.W.—the biggest and solidest organization of labour the United States has ever seen, and you are responsible for its existence and for the present general strike. You smashed all the old federations and drove labour into the I.L.W., and the I.L.W. called the general strike—still fighting for the closed shop. And then you have the effrontery to stand here face to face and tell me that you never got labour down and gouged it. Bah!'

This time there were no denials. Garfield broke out in self-defence:

'We've done nothing we were not compelled to do, if we were to win.'

'I'm not saying anything about that,' Bertie answered. 'What I am complaining about is your squealing now that you're getting a taste of your own medicine. How many strikes have you won by starving labour into submission? Well, labour's worked out a scheme whereby to starve you into submission. It wants the closed shop, and, if it can get it by starving you, why, starve you shall.'

'I notice that you have profited in the past by those very labour gouges you mention,' insinuated Brentwood, one of the wiliest and most astute of our corporation lawyers. 'The receiver is as bad as the thief,' he sneered. 'You had no hand in the gouging, but you took your whack out of the gouge.'

'That is quite beside the question, Brentwood,' Bertie drawled. 'You're as bad as Hanover, intruding the moral element. I haven't said that anything is right or wrong. It's all a rotten game, I know; and my sole kick is that you fellows are squealing now that you're down and labour's taking a gouge out of you. Of course I've taken the profits from the gouging and, thanks to you, gentlemen, without having personally to do the dirty work. You did that for me—oh, believe me, not because I am more virtuous than you, but because my good father and his various brothers left me a lot of money with which to pay for the dirty work.'

'If you mean to insinuate——' Brentwood began hotly.

'Hold on, don't get all—ruffled up,' Bertie interposed insolently. 'There's no use in playing hypocrites in this thieves' den. The high and lofty is all right for the newspapers, boys' clubs, and Sunday schools—that's part of the game; but for heaven's sake don't let's play it on one another. You know, and you know that I know, just what jobbery was done in the building trades' strike last fall, who put up the money, who did the work, and who profited by it.' (Brentwood flushed darkly.) 'But we are all tarred with the same brush, and the best thing for us to do is to leave morality out of it. Again I repeat, play the game, play it to the last finish, but for goodness' sake don't squeal when you get hurt.'

When I left the group Bertie was off on a new tack torment-
ing them with the more serious aspects of the situation,
pointing out the shortage of supplies that was already making
itself felt, and asking them what they were going to do about
it. A little later I met him in the cloak-room, leaving, and
gave him a lift home in my machine.

'It's a great stroke, this general strike,' he said, as we bowled
along through the crowded but orderly streets. 'It's a smashing
body-blow. Labour caught us napping and struck at our
weakest place, the stomach. I'm going to get out of San
Francisco, Corf. Take my advice and get out, too. Head for
the country, anywhere. You'll have more chance. Buy up a
stock of supplies and get into a tent or a cabin somewhere.
Soon there'll be nothing but starvation in this city for such as
we.'

How correct Bertie Messener was I never dreamed. I
decided that he was an alarmist. As for myself, I was content
to remain and watch the fun. After I dropped him, instead of
going directly home, I went on in a hunt for more food. To
my surprise, I learned that the small groceries where I had
bought in the morning were sold out. I extended my search
to the Potrero, and by good luck managed to pick up another
box of candles, two sacks of wheat flour, ten pounds of graham
flour (which would do for the servants), a case of tinned corn,
and two cases of tinned tomatoes. It did look as though there
was going to be at least a temporary food shortage, and I
hugged myself over the goodly stock of provisions I had laid in.

The next morning I had my coffee in bed as usual, and,
more than the cream, I missed the daily paper. It was this
absence of knowledge of what was going on in the world that
I found the chief hardship. Down at the club there was little
news. Rider had crossed from Oakland in his launch, and
Halstead had been down to San Jose and back in his machine.
They reported the same conditions in those places as in San
Francisco. Everything was tied up by the strike. All grocery
stocks had been bought out by the upper classes. And perfect
order reigned. But what was happening over the rest of the

country—in Chicago? New York? Washington? Most probably the same things that were happening with us, we concluded; but the fact that we did not know with absolute surety
was irritating.

General Folsom had a bit of news. An attempt had been
made to place army telegraphers in the telegraph offices, but
the wires had been cut in every direction. This was, so far,
the one unlawful act committed by labour, and that it was a
concerted act he was fully convinced. He had communicated
by wireless with the army post at Benicia, the telegraph lines
were even then being patrolled by soldiers all the way to
Sacramento. Once, for one short instant, they had got the
Sacramento call, then the wires, somewhere, were cut again.
General Folsom reasoned that similar attempts to open communication were being made by the authorities all the way
across the continent, but he was noncommittal as to whether
or not he thought the attempt would succeed. What worried
him was the wire-cutting; he could not but believe that it was
an important part of the deep-laid labour conspiracy. Also, he
regretted that the Government had not long since established
its projected chain of wireless stations.

The days came and went, and for a while it was a humdrum
time. Nothing happened. The edge of excitement had become
blunted. The streets were not so crowded. The working class
did not come uptown any more to see how we were taking the
strike. And there were not so many automobiles running
around. The repair-shops and garages were closed, and whenever a machine broke down it went out of commission. The
clutch on mine broke, and neither love nor money could get it
repaired. Like the rest, I was now walking. San Francisco lay
dead, and we did not know what was happening over the rest
of the country. But from the very fact that we did not know we
could conclude only that the rest of the country lay as dead as
San Francisco. From time to time the city was placarded with
the proclamations of organized labour—these had been printed
months before, and evidenced how thoroughly the I.L.W. had
prepared for the strike. Every detail had been worked out long

in advance. No violence had occurred as yet, with the exception of the shooting of a few wire-cutters by the soldiers, but the people of the slums were starving and growing ominously restless.

The business men, the millionaires, and the professional class held meetings and passed resolutions, but there was no way of making the proclamations public. They could not even get them printed. One result of these meetings, however, was that General Folsom was persuaded into taking military possession of the wholesale houses and of all the flour, grain, and food warehouses. It was high time, for suffering was becoming acute in the homes of the rich, and breadlines were necessary. I knew that my servants were beginning to draw long faces, and it was amazing—the hole they made in my stock of provisions. In fact, as I afterwards surmised, each servant was stealing from me and secreting a private stock of provisions for himself.

But with the formation of the bread-lines came new troubles. There was only so much of a food reserve in San Francisco, and at the best it could not last long. Organized labour, we knew, had its private supplies; nevertheless, the whole working class joined the bread-lines. As a result, the provisions General Folsom had taken possession of diminished with perilous rapidity. How were the soldiers to distinguish between a shabby middle-class man, a member of the I.L.W., or a slum dweller? The first and the last had to be fed, but the soldiers did not know all the I.L.W. men in the city, much less the wives and sons and daughters of the I.L.W. men. The employers helping, a few of the known union men were flung out of the bread-lines; but that amounted to nothing. To make matters worse, the Government tugs that had been hauling food from the army depots on Mare Island to Angel Island found no more food to haul. The soldiers now received their rations from the confiscated provisions, and they received them first.

The beginning of the end was in sight. Violence was beginning to show its face. Law and order were passing away, and passing away, I must confess, among the slum people and the upper classes. Organized labour still maintained perfect order. It could well afford to—it had plenty to eat. I remember the afternoon at the club when I caught Halstead and Brentwood whispering in a corner. They took me in on the venture. Brentwood's machine was still in running order, and they were going out cow-stealing. Halstead had a long butcher knife and a cleaver. We went out to the outskirts of the city. Here and there were cows grazing, but always they were guarded by their owners. We pursued our quest, following along the fringe of the city to the east, and on the hills near Hunter's Point we came upon a cow guarded by a little girl. There was also a young calf with the cow. We wasted no time on preliminaries. The little girl ran away screaming, while we slaughtered the cow. I omit the details, for they are not nice—we were unaccustomed to such work, and we bungled it.

But in the midst of it, working with the haste of fear, we heard cries, and we saw a number of men running towards us. We abandoned the spoils and took to our heels. To our surprise we were not pursued. Looking back, we saw the men hurriedly cutting up the cow. They had been on the same lay as ourselves. We argued that there was plenty for all, and ran back. The scene that followed beggars description. We fought and squabbled over the division like savages. Brentwood, I remember, was a perfect brute, snarling and snapping and threatening that murder would be done if we did not get our proper share.

And we were getting our share when there occurred a new irruption on the scene. This time it was the dreaded peace officers of the I.L.W. The little girl had brought them. They were armed with whips and clubs, and there were a score of them. The little girl danced up and down in anger, the tears streaming down her cheeks, crying: 'Give it to 'em! Give it to 'em! That guy with the specs—he did it! Mash his face for him! Mash his face!' That guy with the specs was I, and I got my face mashed, too, though I had the presence of mind to take off my glasses at the first. My! but we did receive a trouncing as we scattered in all directions. Brentwood, Halstead and I fled away for the machine. Brentwood's nose was bleeding, while Halstead's cheek was cut across with the scarlet slash of a black-snake whip.

And lo, when the pursuit ceased and we had gained the machine, there, hiding behind it, was the frightened calf. Brentwood warned us to be cautious, and crept up on it like a wolf or a tiger. Knife and cleaver had been left behind, but Brentwood still had his hands, and over and over on the ground he rolled with the poor little calf as he throttled it. We threw the carcass into the machine, covered it over with a robe, and started for home. But our misfortunes had only begun. We blew out a tyre. There was no way of fixing it, and twilight was coming on. We abandoned the machine, Brentwood puffing and staggering along in advance, the calf, covered by the robe, slung across his shoulders. We took turn about carrying that calf, and it nearly killed us. Also, we lost our way. And then, after hours of wandering and toil, we encountered a gang of hoodlums. They were not I.L.W. men, and I guess they were as hungry as we. At any rate, they got the calf and we got the thrashing. Brentwood raged like a madman the rest of the way home, and he looked like one, with his torn clothes, swollen nose, and blackened eyes.

There wasn't any more cow-stealing after that. General Folsom sent his troopers out and confiscated all the cows, and his troopers, aided by the militia, ate most of the meat. General Folsom was not to be blamed; it was his duty to maintain law and order, and he maintained it by means of the soldiers, wherefore he was compelled to feed them first of all.

It was about this time that the great panic occurred. The wealthy classes precipitated the flight, and then the slum people caught the contagion and stampeded wildly out of the city. General Folsom was pleased. It was estimated that at least 200,000 had deserted San Francisco, and by that much was his food problem solved. Well do I remember that day. In the morning I had eaten a crust of bread. Half the afternoon I had stood in the bread-line; and after dark I returned home, tired and miserable, carrying a quart of rice and a slice of bacon. Brown met me at the door. His face was worn and terrified. All the servants had fled, he informed me. He alone remained. I was touched by his faithfulness and, when I learned that he had eaten nothing all day, I divided my food with him. We cooked half the rice and half the bacon, sharing it equally and reserving the other half for morning. I went to bed with my hunger, and tossed restlessly all night. In the morning I found Brown had deserted me, and, greater misfortune still, he had stolen what remained of the rice and bacon.

It was a gloomy handful of men that came together at the club that morning. There was no service at all. The last servant was gone. I noticed, too, that the silver was gone, and I learned where it had gone. The servants had not taken it, for the reason, I presume, that the club members got to it first. Their method of disposing of it was simple. Down south of Market Street, in the dwellings of the I.L.W., the housewives had given square meals in exchange for it. I went back to my house. Yes, my silver was gone—all but a massive pitcher. This I wrapped up and carried down south of Market Street.

I felt better after the meal, and returned to the club to learn if there was anything new in the situation. Hanover, Collins and Dakon were just leaving. There was no one inside, they told me, and they invited me to come along with them. They were leaving the city, they said, on Dakon's horses, and there was a spare one for me. Dakon had four magnificent carriage horses that he wanted to save, and General Folsom had given him the tip that next morning all the horses that remained in the city were to be confiscated for food. There were not many horses left, for tens of thousands of them had been turned loose into the country when the hay and grain gave out during the first days. Birdall, I remember, who had great draying interests, had turned loose three hundred dray horses. At an average value of five hundred dollars, this had amounted to $150,000. He had hoped, at first to recover most of the horses after the strike was over, but in the end he never recovered one of them. They were all eaten by the people that fled from San Francisco.

For that matter, the killing of the army mules and horses for food had already begun.

Fortunately for Dakon, he had had a plentiful supply of hay and grain stored in his stable. We managed to raise four saddles, and we found the animals in good condition and spirited, withal unused to being ridden. I remembered the San Francisco of the great earthquake as we rode through the streets, but this San Francisco was vastly more pitiable. No cataclysm of nature had caused this, but, rather, the tyranny of the labour unions. We rode down past Union Square and through the theatre, hotel, and shopping districts. The streets were deserted. Here and there stood automobiles, abandoned where they had broken down or when the gasoline had given out. There was no sign of life, save for the occasional policeman and the soldiers guarding the banks and public buildings. Once we came upon an I.L.W. man pasting up the latest proclamation. We stopped to read. 'We have maintained an orderly strike,' it ran; 'and we shall maintain order to the end. The end will come when our demands are satisfied, and our demands will be satisfied when we have starved our employers into submission, as we ourselves in the past have often been starved into submission.'

'Messener's very words,' Collins said. 'And I, for one, am ready to submit, only they won't give me a chance to submit. I haven't had a full meal in an age. I wonder what horse-meat tastes like?'

We stopped to read another proclamation: 'When we think our employers are ready to submit we shall open up the telegraphs and place the employers' associations of the United States in communication. But only messages relating to peace terms shall be permitted over the wires.'

We rode on, crossed Market Street, and a little later were passing through the working-class district. Here the streets were not deserted. Leaning over the gates or standing in groups were the I.L.W. men. Happy, well-fed children were playing games, and stout housewives sat on the front steps gossiping. One and all cast amused glances at us. Little children ran after us, crying: 'Hey, mister, ain't you hungry?' And one woman, nursing a child at her breast, called to Dakon: 'Say, Fatty, I'll give you a meal for your skate—ham and potatoes, currant jelly, white bread, canned butter, and two cups of coffee.'

'Have you noticed, the last few days,' Hanover remarked to me, 'that there's not been a stray dog in the streets?'

I had noticed, but I had not thought about it before. It was high time to leave the unfortunate city. We at last managed to connect with the San Bruno Road, along which we headed south. I had a country place near Menlo, and it was our objective. But soon we began to discover that the country was worse off and far more dangerous than the city. There the soldiers and the I.L.W. kept order; but the country had been turned over to anarchy. Two hundred thousand people had fled from San Francisco, and we had countless evidences that their flight had been like that of an army of locusts.

They had swept everything clean. There had been robbery and fighting. Here and there we passed bodies by the roadside and saw the blackened ruins of farm-houses. The fences were down, and the crops had been trampled by the feet of a multitude. All the vegetable patches had been rooted up by the famished hordes. All the chickens and farm animals had been slaughtered. This was true of all the main roads that led out of San Francisco. Here and there, away from the roads, farmers had held their own with shotguns and revolvers, and were still holding their own. They warned us away and refused to parley with us. And all the destruction and violence had been done by the slum-dwellers and the upper classes. The I.L.W. men, with plentiful food supplies, remained quietly in their homes in the cities.

Early in the ride we received concrete proof of how desperate was the situation. To the right of us we heard cries and rifle-shots. Bullets whistled dangerously near. There was a crashing in the underbrush; then a magnificent black truck-horse broke across the road in front of us and was gone. We had barely time to notice that he was bleeding and lame. He was followed by three soldiers. The chase went on among the trees on the left. We could hear the soldiers calling to one another. A fourth soldier limped out upon the road from the right, sat down on a boulder, and mopped the sweat from his face.

'Militia,' Dakon whispered. 'Deserters.'

The man grinned up at us and asked for a match. In reply to Dakon's 'What's the word?' he informed us that the militiamen were deserting. 'No grub,' he explained. 'They're feedin' it all to the regulars.' We also learned from him that the military prisoners had been released from Alcatraz Island because they could no longer be fed.

I shall never forget the next sight we encountered. We came upon it abruptly around a turn of the road. Overhead arched the trees. The sunshine was filtering down through the branches. Butterflies were fluttering by, and from the fields came the song of larks. And there it stood, a powerful touring car. About it and in it lay a number of corpses. It told its own tale. Its occupants, fleeing from the city, had been attacked and dragged down by a gang of slum-dwellers—hoodlums. The thing had occurred within twenty-four hours. Freshly opened meat and fruit tins explained the reason for the attack. Dakon examined the bodies.

'I thought so,' he reported. 'I've ridden in that car. It was Perriton—the whole family. We've got to watch out for ourselves from now on.'

'But we have no food with which to invite attack,' I objected.

Dakon pointed to the horse I rode, and I understood.

Early in the day Dakon's horse had cast a shoe. The delicate hoof had split, and by noon the animal was limping. Dakon refused to ride it farther, and refused to desert it. So, on his solicitation, we went on. He would lead the horse and join us at my place. That was the last we saw of him; nor did we ever learn his end.

By one o'clock we arrived at the town of Menlo, or, rather, at the site of Menlo, for it was in ruins. Corpses lay everywhere. The business part of the town, as well as part of the residences had been gutted by fire. Here and there a residence still held

out; but there was no getting near them. When we approached
too closely we were fired upon. We met a woman who was
poking about in the smoking ruins of her cottage. The first
attack, she told us, had been on the stores, and as she talked
we could picture that raging, roaring, hungry mob flinging
itself on the handful of townspeople. Millionaires and paupers
had fought side by side for the food, and then fought with one
another after they got it. The town of Palo Alto and Stanford
University had been sacked in similar fashion, we learned.
Ahead of us lay a desolate, wasted land; and we thought we
were wise in turning off to my place. It lay three miles to the
west, snuggling among the first rolling swells of the foothills.

But as we rode along we saw that the devastation was not
confined to the main roads. The van of the flight had kept to
the roads, sacking the small towns as it went; while those that
followed had scattered out and swept the whole countryside
like a great broom. My place was built of concrete, masonry
and tiles, and so had escaped being burned, but it was gutted
clean. We found the gardener's body in the windmill, littered
around with empty shot-gun shells. He had put up a good
fight. But no trace could we find of the two Italian labourers,
nor of the housekeeper and her husband. Not a live thing
remained. The calves, the colts, all the fancy poultry and
thoroughbred stock, everything, was gone. The kitchen and
the fireplaces, where the mob had cooked, were a mess, while
many campfires outside bore witness to the large number that
had fed and spent the night. What they had not eaten they
had carried away. There was not a bite for us.

We spent the rest of the night vainly waiting for Dakon,
and in the morning, with our revolvers, fought off half a dozen
marauders. Then we killed one of Dakon's horses, hiding for
the future what meat we did not immediately eat. In the
afternoon Collins went out for a walk, but failed to return.
This was the last straw to Hanover. He was for flight there and
then, and I had great difficulty in persuading him to wait for
daylight. As for myself, I was convinced that the end of the
general strike was near, and I was resolved to return to San

Francisco. So, in the morning, we parted company, Hanover heading south, fifty pounds of horse-meat strapped to his saddle, while I, similarly loaded, headed north. Little Hanover pulled through all right, and to the end of his life he will persist, I know, in boring everybody with the narrative of his subsequent adventures.

I got as far as Belmont, on the main road back, when I was robbed of my horse-meat by three militiamen. There was no change in the situation, they said, except that it was going from bad to worse. The I.L.W. had plenty of provisions hidden away and could last out for months. I managed to get as far as Baden, when my horse was taken away from me by a dozen men. Two of them were San Francisco policemen, and the remainder were regular soldiers. This was ominous. The situation was certainly extreme when the regulars were beginning to desert. When I continued my way on foot, they already had the fire started, and the last of Dakon's horses lay slaughtered on the ground.

As luck would have it, I sprained my ankle, and succeeded in getting no farther than South San Francisco. I lay there that night in an outhouse, shivering with the cold and at the same time burning with fever. Two days I lay there, too sick to move, and on the third, reeling and giddy, supporting myself on an extemporized crutch, I tottered on towards San Francisco. I was weak as well, for it was the third day since food had passed my lips. It was a day of nightmare and torment. As in a dream I passed hundreds of regular soldiers drifting along in the opposite direction, and many policemen, with their families, organized in large groups for mutual protection.

As I entered the city I remembered the workman's house at which I had traded the silver pitcher, and in that direction my hunger drove me. Twilight was falling when I came to the place. I passed around by the alleyway and crawled up the back steps, on which I collapsed. I managed to reach out with the crutch and knock on the door. Then I must have fainted, for I came to in the kitchen, my face wet with water, and whisky being poured down my throat. I choked and spluttered and tried to talk. I began saying something about not having any more silver pitchers, but that I would make it up to them afterwards if they would only give me something to eat. But the housewife interrupted me.

'Why, you poor man,' she said, 'haven't you heard? The strike was called off this afternoon. Of course we'll give you something to eat.'

She bustled around, opening a tin of breakfast bacon and preparing to fry it.

'Let me have some now, please,' I begged; and I ate the raw bacon on a slice of bread, while her husband explained that the demands of the I.L.W. had been granted. The wires had been opened up in the early afternoon, and everywhere the employers' associations had given in. There hadn't been any employers left in San Francisco, but General Folsom had spoken for them. The trains and steamers would start running in the morning, and so would everything else just as soon as system could be established.

And that was the end of the general strike. I never want to see another one. It was worse than a war. A general strike is a cruel and immoral thing, and the brain of man should be capable of running industry in a more rational way. Harrison is still my chauffeur. It was part of the conditions of the I.L.W. that all of its members should be reinstated in their old positions. Brown never came back, but the rest of the servants are with me. I hadn't the heart to discharge them—poor creatures, they were pretty hard-pressed when they deserted with the food and silver. And now I can't discharge them. They have all been unionized by the I.L.W. The tyranny of organized labour is getting beyond endurance. Something must be done.

The Men of Forty-Mile

WHEN Big Jim Belden ventured the apparently innocuous proposition that mush-ice was 'rather pecooliar' he little dreamed of what it would lead to. Neither did Lon McFane, when he affirmed that anchor-ice was even more so; nor did Bettles, as he instantly disagreed, declaring the very existence of such a form to be a bugaboo.

'An' ye'd be tellin' me this,' cried Lon, 'after the years ye've spint in the land! An' we atin' out the same pot this many's the day!'

'But the thing's agin reason,' insisted Bettles. 'Look you, water's warmer than ice——'

'An' little the difference, once ye break through.'

'Still it's warmer, because it ain't froze. An' you say it freezes on the bottom?'

'Only the anchor-ice, David, only the anchor-ice. An' have ye niver drifted along, the water clear as glass, whin suddin, belike a cloud over the sun, the mushy-ice comes bubblin' up an' up, till from bank to bank an' bind to bind it's drapin' the river like a first snowfall?'

'Unh, hunh! More'n once when I took a doze at the steering-oar. But it allus come out the nighest sidechannel, an' not bubblin' up an' up.'

'But with niver a wink at the helm?'

'No; nor you. It's agin reason. I'll leave it to any man!'

Bettles appealed to the circle about the stove, but the fight was on between himself and Lon McFane.

'Reason or no reason, it's the truth I'm tellin' ye. Last fall, a year agone, 'twas Sitka Charley and meself saw the sight, droppin' down the riffle ye'll remember below Fort Reliance. An' regular fall weather it was—the glint o' the sun on the golden larch an' the quakin' aspens; an' the glister of light on ivery ripple; an' beyand, the winter an' the blue haze of the north comin' down hand in hand. It's well ye know the same, with a fringe to the river an' the ice formin' thick in the eddies—an' a snap an' sparkle to the air, an' ye a-feelin' it through all yer blood, a-takin' new lease of life with ivery suck of it. 'Tis then, me boy, the world grows small an' the wandtherlust lays ye by the heels.

'But it's meself as wandthers. As I was sayin', we a-paddlin', with niver a sign of ice, barrin' that by the eddies, when the Injin lifts his paddle an' sings out, "Lon McFane! Look ye below! So have I heard, but niver thought to see!" As ye know, Sitka Charley, like meself, niver drew first breath in the land; so the sight was new. Then we drifted, with a head over ayther side, peerin' down through the sparkly water. For the world like the days I spint with the pearlers, watchin' the coral banks a-growin' the same as so many gardens under the sea. There it was, the anchor-ice, clingin' and clusterin' to ivery rock, after the manner of the white coral.

'But the best of the sight was to come. Just after clearin' the tail of the riffle, the water turns quick the colour of milk, an' the top of it in wee circles, as when the graylin' rise in the spring, or there's a splatter of wet from the sky. 'Twas the anchor-ice comin' up. To the right, to the lift, as far as iver a man cud see, the water was covered with the same. An' like so much porridge it was, slickin' along the bark of the canoe, stickin' like glue to the paddles. It's many's the time I shot the self-same riffle before, and it's many's the time after, but niver a wink of the same have I seen. 'Twas the sight of a lifetime.'

'Do tell!' dryly commented Bettles. 'D'ye think I'd b'lieve such a yarn? I'd ruther say the glister of light'd gone to your eyes, and the snap of the air to your tongue.'

''Twas me own eyes that beheld it, an' if Sitka Charley was here, he'd be the lad to back me.'

'But facts is facts, an' they ain't no gettin' round 'em. It ain't in the nature of things for the water fartherest away from the air to freeze first.'

'But me own eyes——'

'Don't git het up over it,' admonished Bettles, as the quick Celtic anger began to mount.

'Then yer not after belavin' me?'

'Sence you're so blamed forehanded about it, no; I'd b'lieve nature first, and facts.'

'Is it the lie ye'd be givin' me?' threatened Lon. 'Ye'd better be askin' that Siwash wife of yours. I'll lave it to her, for the truth I spake.'

Bettles flared up in sudden wrath. The Irishman had unwittingly wounded him; for his wife was the half-breed daughter of a Russian fur-trader, married to him in the Greek Mission of Nulato, a thousand miles or so down the Yukon, thus being of much higher caste than the common Siwash, or native, wife. It was a mere Northland nuance, which none but the Northland adventurer may understand.

'I reckon you kin take it that way,' was his deliberate affirmation.

The next instant Lon McFane had stretched him on the floor, the circle was broken up, and half a dozen men had stepped between.

Bettles came to his feet, wiping the blood from his mouth. 'It hain't new, this takin' and payin' of blows, and don't you never think but that this will be squared.'

'An' niver in me life did I take the lie from mortal man,' was the retort courteous. 'An' it's an avil day I'll not be to hand waitin' and' willin' to help ye lift yer debts, barrin' no manner of way.'

'Still got that 38·55?'

Lon nodded.

'But you'd better git a more likely calibre. Mine'll rip holes through you the size of walnuts.'

'Niver fear; it's me own slugs smell their way with soft noses, an' they spread like flapjacks against the coming out beyand. An' when'll I have the pleasure of waitin' on ye? The water-hole's a strikin' locality.'

'`T aint bad. Jest be there in an hour, and you won't set long on my coming.'

Both men mittened and left the Post, their ears closed to the remonstrances of their comrades. It was such a little thing; yet with such men, little things, nourished by quick tempers and stubborn natures, soon blossomed into big things. Besides, the art of burning to bed-rock still lay in the womb of the future, and the men of Forty-Mile, shut in by the long Arctic winter, grew high-stomached with overeating and enforced idleness, and became as irritable as do the bees in the fall of the year when the hives are overstocked with honey.

There was no law in the land. The mounted police was also a thing of the future. Each man measured an offence, and meted out the punishment inasmuch as it affected himself. Rarely had combined action been necessary, and never in all the dreary history of the camp had the eighth article of the Decalogue been violated.

Big Jim Belden called an impromptu meeting. Scruff Mackenzie was placed as temporary chairman, and a messenger dispatched to solicit Father Roubeau's good offices. Their position was paradoxical, and they knew it. By the right of might could they interfere to prevent the duel; yet such action, while in direct line with their wishes, went counter to their opinions. While their rough-hewn, obsolete ethics recognized the individual prerogative of wiping out blow with blow, they could not bear to think of two good comrades, such as Bettles and McFane, meeting in deadly battle. Deeming the man who would not fight on provocation a dastard, when brought to the test it seemed wrong that he should fight.

But a scurry of moccasins and loud cries, rounded off with a pistol-shot, interrupted the discussion. Then the storm-doors opened and Malemute Kid entered, a smoking Colt in his hand, and a merry light in his eye.

'I got him.' He replaced the empty shell, and added, 'Your dog, Scruff.'

'Yellow Fang?' Mackenzie asked.

'No; the lop-eared one.'

'The devil! Nothing the matter with him.'

'Come out and take a look.'

'That's all right after all. Guess he's got 'em, too. Yellow Fang came back this morning and took a chunk out of him, and came near to making a widower of me. Made a rush for Zarinska, but she whisked her skirts in his face and escaped with the loss of the same and a good roll in the snow. Then he took to the woods again. Hope he don't come back. Lost any yourself?'

'One—the best one of the pack—Shookum. Started amuck this morning, but didn't get very far. Ran foul of Sitka Charley's team, and they scattered him all over the street. And now two of them are loose, and raging mad; so you see he got his work in. The dog census will be small in the spring if we don't do something.'

'And the man census, too.'

'How's that? Who's in trouble now?'

'Oh, Bettles and Lon McFane had an argument, and they'll be down by the water-hole in a few minutes to settle it.'

The incident was repeated for his benefit, and Malemute Kid, accustomed to an obedience which his fellow men never failed to render, took charge of the affair. His quickly formulated plan was explained, and they promised to follow his lead implicitly.

'So you see,' he concluded, 'we do not actually take away their privilege of fighting; and yet I don't believe they'll fight when they see the beauty of the scheme. Life's a game, and men the gamblers. They'll stake their whole pile on the one chance in a thousand. Take away that one chance, and—they won't play.'

He turned to the man in charge of the Post. 'Storekeeper, weigh out three fathoms of your best half-inch manila.'

'We'll establish a precedent which will last the men of Forty-Mile to the end of time,' he prophesied. Then he coiled the rope about his arm and led his followers out of doors, just in time to meet the principals.

'What danged right'd he to fetch my wife in?' thundered Bettles to the soothing overtures of a friend. ''Twa'n't called for,' he concluded decisively. ''Twa'n't called for,' he reiterated again and again, pacing up and down and waiting for Lon McFane.

L

And Lon McFane—his face was hot and tongue rapid as he flaunted insurrection in the face of the Church. 'Then, father,' he cried, 'it's with an aisy heart I'll roll in me flamy blankets, the broad of me back on a bed of coals. Niver shall it be said Lon McFane took a lie 'twixt the teeth without iver liftin' a hand! An' I'll not ask a blessin'. The years have been wild, but it's the heart was in the right place.'

'But it's not the heart, Lon,' interposed Father Roubeau; 'It's pride that bids you forth to slay your fellow man.'

'Yer Frinch,' Lon replied. And then, turning to leave him, 'An' will ye say a mass if the luck is against me?'

But the priest smiled, thrust his moccasined feet to the fore, and went out upon the white breast of the silent river. A packed trail, the width of a sixteen-inch sled, led out to the water-hole. On either side lay the deep, soft snow. The men trod in single file, without conversation; and the black-stoled priest in their midst gave to the function the solemn aspect of a funeral. It was a warm winter's day for Forty-Mile—a day in which the sky, filled with heaviness, drew closer to the earth, and the mercury sought the unwonted level of twenty below. But there was no cheer in the warmth. There was little air in the upper strata, and the clouds hung motionless, giving sullen promise of an early snowfall. And the earth, unresponsive, made no preparation, content in its hibernation.

When the water-hole was reached, Bettles, having evidently reviewed the quarrel during the silent walk, burst out in a final "Twa'n't called for,' while Lon McFane kept grim silence. Indignation so choked him that he could not speak.

Yet deep down, whenever their own wrongs were not uppermost, both men wondered at their comrades. They had expected opposition, and this tacit acquiescence hurt them. It seemed more was due them from the men they had been so close with, and they felt a vague sense of wrong, rebelling at the thought of so many of their brothers coming out, as on a gala occasion, without one word of protest, to see them shoot each other down. It appeared their worth had diminished in the eyes of the community. The proceedings puzzled them.

'Back to back, David. An' will it be fifty paces to the man, or double the quantity?'

'Fifty,' was the sanguinary reply, grunted out, yet sharply cut.

But the new manila, not prominently displayed, but casually coiled about Malemute Kid's arm, caught the quick eye of the Irishman, and thrilled him with a suspicious fear.

'An' what are ye doin' with the rope?'

'Hurry up!' Malemute Kid glanced at his watch. 'I've a batch of bread in the cabin, and I don't want it to fall. Besides, my feet are getting cold.'

The rest of the men manifested their impatience in various suggestive ways.

'But the rope, Kid? It's bran' new, an' sure yer bread's not that heavy it needs raisin' with the like of that?'

Bettles by this time had faced around. Father Roubeau, the humour of the situation just dawning on him, hid a smile behind his mittened hand.

'No, Lon; this rope was made for a man.' Malemute Kid could be very impressive on occasion.

'What man?' Bettles was becoming aware of a personal interest.

'The other man.'

'An' which is the one ye'd mane by that?'

'Listen, Lon—and you, too, Bettles! We've been talking this little trouble of yours over, and we've come to one conclusion. We know we have no right to stop your fighting——'

'True for ye, me lad!'

'And we're not going to. But this much we can do, and shall do—make this the only duel in the history of Forty-Mile, set an example for every *che-che-qua* that comes up or down the Yukon. The man who escapes killing shall be hanged to the nearest tree. Now, go ahead!'

Lon smiled dubiously, then his face lighted up. 'Pace her off, David—fifty paces, wheel, an' niver a cease firin' till a lad's down for good. 'Tis their heart's'll niver let them do the deed, an' it's well ye should know it for a true Yankee bluff.'

He started off with a pleased grin on his face, but Malemute Kid halted him.

'Lon! It's a long while since you first knew me?'

'Many's the day.'

'And you, Bettles?'

'Five year next June high water.'

'And have you once, in all that time, known me to break my word? Or heard of me breaking it?'

Both men shook their heads, striving to fathom what lay beyond.

'Well, then, what do you think of a promise made by me?'

'As good as your bond,' from Bettles.

'The thing to safely sling yer hopes of heaven by,' promptly endorsed Lon McFane.

'Listen! I, Malemute Kid, give you my word—and you know what that means—that the man who is not shot stretches rope within ten minutes after the shooting.' He stepped back as Pilate might have done after washing his hands.

A pause and a silence came over the men of Forty-Mile. The sky drew closer, sending down a crystal flight of frost—little geometric designs, perfect, evanescent as a breath, yet destined to exist till the returning sun had covered half its northern journey. Both men had led forlorn hopes in their time—led, with a curse or a jest on their tongues, and in their souls an unswerving faith in the God of Chance. But that merciful deity had been shut out from the present deal. They studied the face of Malemute Kid, but they studied as one might the Sphinx. As the quiet minutes passed, a feeling that speech was incumbent on them began to grow. At last the howl of a wolf-dog cracked the silence from the direction of Forty-Mile. The weird sound swelled with all the pathos of a breaking heart, then died away in a long-drawn sob.

'Well I be danged!' Bettles turned up the collar of his mackinaw jacket and stared about him helplessly.

'It's a gloryus game yer runnin', Kid,' cried Lon McFane.

'All the percentage to the house an' niver a bit to the man that's buckin'. The Devil himself'd niver tackle such a cinch—and damned if I do.'

There were chuckles, throttled in gurgling throats, and winks brushed away with the frost which rimed the eyelashes, as the men climbed the ice-notched bank and started across the street to the Post. But the long howl had drawn nearer, invested with a new note of menace. A woman screamed round the corner. There was a cry of, 'Here he comes!' Then an Indian boy, at the head of half a dozen frightened dogs, racing with death, dashed into the crowd. And behind came Yellow Fang, a bristle of hair and a flash of grey. Everybody but the Yankee fled. The Indian boy had tripped and fallen. Bettles stopped long enough to grip him by the slack of his furs, then headed for a pile of cordwood already occupied by a number of his comrades. Yellow Fang, doubling after one of the dogs, came leaping back. The fleeing animal, free of the rabies, but crazed with fright, whipped Bettles off his feet and flashed on up the street. Malemute Kid took a flying shot at Yellow Fang. The mad dog whirled a half airspring, came down on his back, then, with a single leap, covered half the distance between himself and Bettles.

But the fatal spring was intercepted. Lon McFane leaped from the woodpile, countering him in mid-air. Over they rolled, Lon holding him by the throat at arm's length, blinking under the fetid slaver which sprayed his face. Then Bettles, revolver in hand and coolly waiting a chance, settled the combat.

''Twas a square game, Kid,' Lon remarked, rising to his feet and shaking the snow from out of his sleeves; 'with a fair percentage to meself that bucked it.'

That night, while Lon McFane sought the forgiving arms of the Church in the direction of Father Roubeau's cabin, Malemute Kid talked long to little purpose.

'But would you,' persisted Mackenzie, 'supposing they had fought?'

'Have I ever broken my word?'

'No; but that isn't the point. Answer the question. Would you?'

Malemute Kid straightened up. 'Scruff, I've been asking myself that question ever since, and——'

'Well?'

'Well, as yet, I haven't found the answer.'

A Piece of Steak

WITH the last morsel of bread Tom King wiped his plate clean of the last particle of flour gravy and chewed the resulting mouthful in a slow and meditative way. When he arose from the table, he was oppressed by the feeling that he was distinctly hungry. Yet he alone had eaten. The two children in the other room had been sent early to bed in order that in sleep they might forget they had gone supperless. His wife had touched nothing, and had sat silently and watched him with solicitous eyes. She was a thin, worn woman of the working class, though signs of an earlier prettiness were not wanting in her face. The flour for the gravy she had borrowed from the neighbour across the hall. The last two ha'pennies had gone to buy the bread.

He sat down by the window on a rickety chair that protested under his weight, and quite mechanically he put his pipe in his mouth and dipped into the side pocket of his coat. The absence of any tobacco made him aware of his action, and with a scowl for his forgetfulness he put the pipe away. His movements were slow, almost hulking, as though he were burdened by the heavy weight of his muscles. He was a solid-bodied, stolid-looking man, and his appearance did not suffer from being over-prepossessing. His rough clothes were old and slouchy. The uppers of his shoes were too weak to carry the heavy resoling that was itself of no recent date. And his cotton shirt, a cheap, two-shilling affair, showed a frayed collar and ineradicable paint stains.

But it was Tom King's face that advertised him unmistakably for what he was. It was the face of a typical prize-fighter; of one who had put in long years of service in the squared ring, and, by that means, developed and emphasized all the marks of the fighting beast. It was distinctly a lowering countenance, and, that no feature of it might escape notice, it was clean-shaven. The lips were shapeless and constituted a mouth harsh to excess, that was like a gash in his face. The jaw was aggressive, brutal, heavy. The eyes, slow of movement and heavy-lidded, were almost expressionless under the shaggy, indrawn brows. Sheer animal that he was, the eyes were the most animal-like feature about him. They were sleepy, lion-like—the eyes of a fighting animal. The forehead slanted quickly back to the hair, which, clipped close, showed every bump of a villainous-looking head. A nose, twice broken and moulded variously by countless blows, and a cauliflower ear, permanently swollen and distorted to twice its size, completed his adornment, while the beard, fresh-shaven as it was, sprouted in the skin and gave the face a blue-black stain.

Altogether, it was the face of a man to be afraid of in a dark alley or lonely place. And yet Tom King was not a criminal, nor had he ever done anything criminal. Outside of brawls, common to his walk in life, he had harmed no one. Nor had he ever been known to pick a quarrel. He was a professional, and all the fighting brutishness of him was reserved for his professional appearances. Outside the ring he was slow-going, easy-natured, and, in his younger days, when money was flush, too open-handed for his own good. He bore no grudges and had few enemies. Fighting was a business with him. In the ring he struck to hurt, struck to maim, struck to destroy; but there was no animus in it. It was a plain business proposition. Audiences assembled and paid for the spectacle of men knocking each other out. The winner took the big end of the purse. When Tom King faced the Woolloomoolloo Gouger, twenty years before, he knew that the Gouger's jaw was only four months healed after having been broken in a Newcastle bout. And he had played for that jaw and broken it again in the ninth round, not because he bore the Gouger any ill will, but because that was the surest way to put the Gouger out and win the big end of the purse. Nor had the Gouger borne him any ill will for it. It was the game, and both knew the game and played it.

Tom King had never been a talker, and he sat by the window, morosely silent, staring at his hands. The veins stood out on the backs of the hands, large and swollen; and the knuckles smashed and battered and malformed, testified to the use to which they had been put. He had never heard that a man's life was the life of his arteries, but well he knew the meaning of those big, upstanding veins. His heart had pumped too much blood through them at top pressure. They no longer did the work. He had stretched the elasticity out of them, and with their distension had passed his endurance. He tired easily now. No longer could he do a fast twenty rounds, hammer and tongs, fight, fight, fight, from gong to gong, with fierce rally on top of fierce rally, beaten to the ropes and in turn beating his opponent to the ropes, and rallying fiercest and fastest of all in that last, twentieth round, with the house on its feet and yelling, himself rushing, striking, ducking, raining showers of blows upon showers of blows and receiving showers of blows in return, and all the time the heart faithfully pumping the surging blood through the adequate veins. The veins, swollen at the time, had always shrunk down again, though not quite— each time, imperceptibly at first, remaining just a trifle larger than before. He stared at them and at his battered knuckles, and, for the moment, caught a vision of the youthful excellence of those hands before the first knuckle had been smashed on the head of Benny Jones, otherwise known as the Welsh Terror.

The impression of his hunger came back on him.

'Blimey, but couldn't I go a piece of steak!' he muttered aloud, clenching his huge fists and spitting out a smothered oath.

'I tried both Burke's an' Sawley's,' his wife said half apologetically.

'An' they wouldn't?' he demanded.

'Not a ha'penny. Burke said——' She faltered.

'G'wan! Wot'd he say?'

'As how 'e was thinkin' Sandel 'ud do ye tonight, an' as how yer score was uncomfortable big as it was.'

Tom King grunted but did not reply. He was busy thinking of the bull terrier he had kept in his younger days to which he had fed steaks without end. Burke would have given him credit for a thousand steaks—then. But times had changed. Tom

King was getting old; and old men, fighting before second-rate clubs, couldn't expect to run bills of any size with the tradesmen.

He had got up in the morning with a longing for a piece of steak, and the longing had not abated. He had not had a fair training for this fight. It was a drought year in Australia, times were hard, and even the most irregular work was difficult to find. He had had no sparring partner, and his food had not been of the best nor always sufficient. He had done a few days' navvy work when he could get it, and he had run around the Domain in the early mornings to get his legs in shape. But it was hard, training without a partner and with a wife and two kiddies that must be fed. Credit with the tradesmen had undergone very slight expansion when he was matched with Sandel. The secretary of the Gayety Club had advanced him three pounds—the loser's end of the purse—and beyond that had refused to go. Now and again he had managed to borrow a few shillings from old pals, who would have lent more only that it was a drought year and they were hard put themselves. No—and there was no use in disguising the fact—his training had not been satisfactory. He should have had better food and no worries. Besides, when a man is forty, it is harder to get into condition than when he is twenty.

'What time is it, Lizzie?' he asked.

His wife went across the hall to inquire, and came back.

'Quarter before eight.'

'They'll be startin' the first bout in a few minutes,' he said. 'Only a try-out. Then there's a four-round spar 'tween Dealer Wells an' Gridley, an' a ten-round go 'tween Starlight an' some sailor bloke. I don't come on for over an hour.'

At the end of another silent ten minutes he rose to his feet.

'Truth is, Lizzie, I ain't had proper trainin'.'

He reached for his hat and started for the door. He did not offer to kiss her—he never did on going out—but on this night she dared to kiss him, throwing her arms around him and compelling him to bend down to her face. She looked quite small against the massive bulk of the man.

'Good luck, Tom,' she said. 'You gotter do 'im.'

'Ay, I gotter do 'im,' he repeated. 'That's all there is to it. I jus' gotter do 'im.'

He laughed with an attempt at heartiness, while she pressed more closely against him. Across her shoulders he looked around the bare room. It was all he had in the world, with the rent overdue, and her and the kiddies. And he was leaving it to go out into the night to get meat for his mate and cubs—not like a modern working man going to his machine grind, but in the old, primitive, royal, animal way, by fighting for it.

'I gotter do 'im,' he repeated, this time a hint of desperation in his voice. 'If it's a win, it's thirty quid—an' I can pay all that's owin', with a lump o' money left over. If it's a lose, I get naught—not even a penny for me to ride home on the tram. The secretary's give all that's comin' from a loser's end. Good-bye, old woman. I'll come straight home if it's a win.'

'An' I'll be waitin' up,' she called to him along the hall.

It was a full two miles to the Gayety, and as he walked along he remembered how in his palmy days—he had once been the heavyweight champion of New South Wales—he would have ridden in a cab to the fight, and how, most likely, some heavy backer would have paid for the cab and ridden with him. There were Tommy Burns and that Yankee, Jack Johnson— they rode about in motor-cars. And he walked! And, as any man knew, a hard two miles was not the best preliminary to a fight. He was an old 'un, and the world did not wag well with old 'uns. He was good for nothing now except navvy work, and his broken nose and swollen ear were against him even in that. He found himself wishing that he had learned a trade. It would have been better in the long run. But no one had told him, and he knew, deep down in his heart, that he would not have listened if they had. It had been so easy. Big money—sharp, glorious fights—periods of rest and loafing in between—a following of eager flatterers, the slaps on the back, the shakes of the hand, the toffs glad to buy him a drink for the privilege of five minutes' talk—and the glory of it, the yelling houses, the whirlwind finish, the referee's 'King wins!' and his name in the sporting columns next day.

Those had been times! But he realized now, in his slow, ruminating way, that it was the old 'uns he had been putting away. He was Youth, rising; and they were Age, sinking. No wonder it had been easy—they with their swollen veins and battered knuckles and weary in the bones of them from the long battles they had already fought. He remembered the time he put out old Stowsher Bill, at Rush-Cutters Bay, in the eighteenth round, and how old Bill had cried afterwards in the dressing-room like a baby. Perhaps old Bill's rent had been overdue. Perhaps he'd had at home a missus an' a couple of kiddies. And perhaps Bill, that very day of the fight, had had a hungering for a piece of steak. Bill had fought game and taken incredible punishment. He could see now, after he had gone through the mill himself, that Stowsher Bill had fought for a bigger stake, that night twenty years ago, than had young Tom King, who had fought for glory and easy money. No wonder Stowsher Bill had cried afterwards in the dressing-room.

Well, a man had only so many fights in him, to begin with. It was the iron law of the game. One man might have a hundred hard fights in him, another man only twenty; each, according to the make of him and the quality of his fibre, had a definite number, and when he had fought them he was done. Yes, he had had more fights in him than most of them, and he had had far more than his share of the hard, gruelling fights —the kind that worked the heart and lungs to bursting, that took the elastic out of the arteries and made hard knots of muscle out of youth's sleek suppleness, that wore out nerve and stamina and made brain and bones weary from excess of effort and endurance overwrought. Yes, he had done better than all of them. There was none of his old fighting partners left. He was the last of the old guard. He had seen them all finished, and he had had a hand in finishing some of them.

They had tried him out against the old 'uns, and one after another he had put them away—laughing when, like old Stowsher Bill, they cried in the dressing-room. And now he was an old 'un, and they tried out the youngsters on him. There was that bloke Sandel. He had come over from New Zealand with a record behind him. But nobody in Australia knew anything about him, so they put him up against old Tom King. If Sandel made a showing, he would be given better men to fight, with bigger purses to win; so it was to be depended upon that he would put up a fierce battle. He had everything to win by it—money and glory and career; and Tom King was the grizzled old chopping block that guarded the highway to fame and fortune. And he had nothing to win except thirty quid, to pay to the landlord and the tradesmen. And as Tom King thus ruminated, there came to his stolid vision the form of youth, glorious youth, rising exultant and invincible, supple of muscle and silken of skin, with heart and lungs that had never been tired and torn and that laughed at limitation of effort. Yes, youth was the nemesis. It destroyed the old 'uns and recked not that, in so doing, it destroyed itself. It enlarged its arteries and smashed its knuckles, and was in turn destroyed by youth. For youth was ever youthful. It was only age that grew old.

At Castlereagh Street he turned to the left, and three blocks along came to the Gayety. A crowd of young larrikins hanging outside the door made respectful way for him, and he heard one say to another: 'That's 'im! That's Tom King!'

Inside, on the way to his dressing-room, he encountered the secretary, a keen-eyed, shrewd-faced young man, who shook his hand.

'How are you feelin', Tom?' he asked.

'Fit as a fiddle,' King answered, though he knew that he lied, and that if he had a quid he would give it right there for a good piece of steak.

When he emerged from the dressing-room, his seconds behind him, and came down the aisle to the squared ring in the centre of the hall, a burst of greeting and applause went up from the waiting crowd. He acknowledged salutations right and left, though few of the faces did he know. Most of them were the faces of kiddies unborn when he was winning his first laurels in the squared ring. He leaped lightly to the raised platform and ducked through the ropes to his corner, where he sat down on a folding stool. Jack Ball, the referee, came over and shook his hand. Ball was a broken-down pugilist who for over ten years had not entered the ring as a principal. King was glad that he had him for referee. They were both old 'uns. If he should rough it with Sandel a bit beyond the rules, he knew Ball could be depended upon to pass it by.

Aspiring young heavyweights, one after another, were climbing into the ring and being presented to the audience by the referee. Also he issued their challenges for them.

'Young Pronto,' Bill announced, 'from North Sydney, challenges the winner for fifty pounds side bet.'

The audience applauded, and applauded again as Sandel himself sprang through the ropes and sat down in his corner. Tom King looked across the ring at him curiously, for in a few minutes they would be locked together in merciless combat, each trying with all the force of him to knock the other into unconsciousness. But little could he see, for Sandel, like himself, had trousers and sweater on over his ring costume. His face was strongly handsome, crowned with a curly mop of yellow hair, while his thick, muscular neck hinted at bodily magnificence.

Young Pronto went to one corner and then the other, shaking hands with the principals and dropping down out of the ring. The challenges went on. Every youth climbed through the ropes—youth unknown but insatiable, crying out to mankind that with strength and skill it would match issues with the winner. A few years before, in his own hey-day of invincibleness, Tom King would have been amused and bored by these preliminaries. But now he sat fascinated, unable to shake the vision of youth from his eyes. Always were these youngsters rising up in the boxing game, springing through the ropes and shouting their defiance; and always were the old 'uns going down before them. They climbed to success over the bodies of the old 'uns. And ever they came, more and more youngsters—youth unquenchable and irresistible—and ever they put the old 'uns away, themselves becoming old 'uns and travelling the same downward path, while behind them, ever pressing on them, was youth eternal—the new babies, grown lusty and dragging their elders down, with behind them more babies to the end of time—youth that must have its will and that will never die.

King glanced over to the Press box, nodded to Morgan, of the *Sportsman*, and Corbett, of the *Referee*. Then he held out his hands, while Sid Sullivan and Charley Bates, his seconds, slipped on his gloves and laced them tight, closely watched by one of Sandel's seconds, who first examined critically the tapes on King's knuckles. A second of his own was in Sandel's corner, performing a like office. Sandel's trousers were pulled off, and as he stood up his sweater was skinned off over his head. And Tom King, looking, saw youth incarnate, deep-chested, heavy-thewed, with muscles that slipped and slid like live things under the white satin skin. The whole body was acrawl with life, and Tom King knew that it was a life that had never oozed its freshness out through the aching pores during the long fights wherein youth paid its toll and departed not quite so young as when it entered.

The two men advanced to meet each other, and as the gong sounded and the seconds clattered out of the ring with the folding stools, they shook hands and instantly took their fighting attitudes. And instantly, like a mechanism of steel and springs balanced on a hair trigger, Sandel was in and out and in again, landing a left to the eyes, a right to the ribs, ducking a counter, dancing lightly away and dancing menacingly back again. He was swift and clever. It was a dazzling exhibition. The house yelled its approbation. But King was not dazzled. He had fought too many fights and too many youngsters. He knew the blows for what they were—too quick and too deft to be dangerous. Evidently Sandel was going to rush things from the start. It was to be expected. It was the way of youth, expending its splendour and excellence in wild insurgence and furious onslaught, overwhelming opposition with its own unlimited glory of strength and desire.

Sandel was in and out, here, there, and everywhere, light-footed and eager-hearted, a living wonder of white flesh and stinging muscle that wove itself into a dazzling fabric of attack, slipping and leaping like a flying shuttle from action to action through a thousand actions, all of them centred upon the destruction of Tom King, who stood between him and fortune. And Tom King patiently endured. He knew his business, and he knew youth now that youth was no longer his. There was nothing to do till the other lost some of his steam, was his thought, and he grinned to himself as he deliberately ducked so as to receive a heavy blow on the top of his head. It was a wicked thing to do, yet eminently fair according to the rules of the boxing game. A man was supposed to take care of his own knuckles, and if he insisted on hitting an opponent on the top of the head he did so at his own peril. King could have ducked lower and let the blow whizz harmlessly past, but he remembered his own early fights and how he smashed his first knuckle on the head of the Welsh Terror. He was but playing the game. That duck had accounted for one of Sandel's knuckles. Not that Sandel would mind it now. He would go on, superbly regardless, hitting as hard as ever throughout the fight. But later on, when the long ring battles had begun to tell, he would regret that knuckle and look back and remember how he smashed it on Tom King's head.

The first round was all Sandel's, and he had the house yelling with the rapidity of his whirlwind rushes. He overwhelmed King with avalanches of punches, and King did nothing. He never struck once, contenting himself with covering up, blocking and ducking and clinching to avoid punishment. He occasionally feinted, shook his head when the weight of a punch landed, and moved stolidly about, never leaping or springing or wasting an ounce of strength. Sandel must foam the froth of youth away before discreet age could dare to retaliate. All King's movements were slow and methodical, and his heavy-lidded, slow-moving eyes gave him the appearance of being half asleep or dazed. Yet they were eyes that saw everything, that had been trained to see everything through all his twenty years and odd in the ring. They were eyes that did not blink or waver before an impending blow, but that coolly saw and measured distance.

Seated back in his corner for the minute's rest at the end of the round, he lay back with outstretched legs, his arms resting on the right-angle of the ropes, his chest and abdomen heaving frankly and deeply as he gulped down the air driven by the towels of his seconds. He listened with closed eyes to the voices of the house, 'Why don't yeh fight, Tom?' many were crying. 'Yeh ain't afraid of 'im, are yeh?'

'Muscle-bound,' he heard a man on a front seat comment. 'He can't move quicker. Two to one on Sandel, in quids.'

The gong struck and the two men advanced from their corners. Sandel came forward fully three-quarters of the distance, eager to begin again; but King was content to advance the shorter distance. It was in line with his policy of economy. He had not been well trained, and he had not had enough to eat, and every step counted. Besides, he had already walked two miles to the ringside. It was a repetition of the first round, with Sandel attacking like a whirlwind and with the audience indignantly demanding why King did not fight. Beyond feinting and several slowly delivered and ineffectual blows he did nothing save block and stall and clinch. Sandel wanted to make the pace fast, while King, out of his wisdom, refused to accommodate him. He grinned with a certain wistful pathos in his ring-battered countenance, and went on cherishing his strength with the jealousy of which only age is capable. Sandel was youth, and he threw his strength away with the munificent abandon of youth. To King belonged the ring generalship, the wisdom bred of long, aching fights. He watched with cool eyes and head, moving slowly and waiting for Sandel's froth to foam away. To the majority of the onlookers it seemed as though King was hopelessly outclassed, and they voiced their opinion in offers of three to one on Sandel. But there were wise ones, a few, who knew King of old time, and who covered what they considered easy money.

The third round began as usual, one-sided, with Sandel

doing all the leading and delivering all the punishment. A half minute had passed when Sandel, over-confident, left an opening. King's eyes and right arm flashed in the same instant. It was his first real blow—a hook, with the twisted arch of the arm to make it rigid, and with all the weight of the half-pivoted body behind it. It was like a sleepy-seeming lion suddenly thrusting out a lightning paw. Sandel, caught on the side of the jaw, was felled like a bullock. The audience gasped and murmured awe-stricken applause. The man was not muscle-bound, after all, and he could drive a blow like a trip hammer.

Sandel was shaken. He rolled over and attempted to rise, but the sharp yells from his seconds to take the count restrained him. He knelt on one knee, ready to rise, and waited, while the referee stood over him, counting the seconds loudly in his ear. At the ninth he rose in fighting attitude, and Tom King, facing him, knew regret that the blow had not been an inch nearer the point of the jaw. That would have been a knock-out, and he could have carried the thirty quid home to the missus and the kiddies.

The round continued to the end of its three minutes, Sandel for the first time respectful of his opponent and King slow of movement and sleepy-eyed as ever. As the round neared its close, King, warned of the fact by sight of the seconds crouching outside ready for the spring in through the ropes, worked the fight around to his own corner. And when the gong struck, he sat down immediately on the waiting stool, while Sandel had to walk all the way across the diagonal of the square to his own corner. It was a little thing, but it was the sum of little things that counted. Sandel was compelled to walk that many more steps, to give up that much energy, and to lose a part of the precious minute of rest. At the beginning of every round King loafed slowly out from his corner, forcing his opponent to advance the greater distance. The end of every round found the fight manœuvred by King into his own corner so that he could immediately sit down.

Two more rounds went by, in which King was parsimonious

of effort and Sandel prodigal. The latter's attempt to force a fast pace made King uncomfortable, for a fair percentage of the multitudinous blows showered upon him went home. Yet King persisted in his dogged slowness, despite the crying of the young hotheads for him to go in and fight. Again, in the sixth round, Sandel was careless, again Tom King's fearful right flashed out to the jaw, and again Sandel took the nine seconds' count.

By the seventh round Sandel's pink of condition was gone, and he settled down to what he knew was to be the hardest fight in his experience. Tom King was an old 'un, but a better old 'un than he had ever encountered—an old 'un who never lost his head, who was remarkably able at defence, whose blows had the impact of a knotted club, and who had a knock-out in either hand. Nevertheless, Tom King dared not hit often. He never forgot his battered knuckles, and knew that every hit must count if the knuckles were to last out the fight. As he sat in his corner, glancing across at his opponent, the thought came to him that the sum of his wisdom and Sandel's youth would constitute a world's champion heavyweight. But that was the trouble. Sandel would never become a world champion. He lacked the wisdom, and the only way for him to get it was to buy it with youth; and when wisdom was his, youth would have been spent in buying it.

King took every advantage he knew. He never missed an opportunity to clinch, and in effecting most of the clinches his shoulder drove stiffly into the other's ribs. In the philosophy of the ring a shoulder was as good as a punch so far as damage was concerned, and a great deal better so far as concerned expenditure of effort. Also in the clinches King rested his weight on his opponent, and was loath to let go. This compelled the interference of the referee, who tore them apart, always assisted by Sandel, who had not yet learned to rest. He could not refrain from using those glorious flying arms and writhing muscles of his, and when the other rushed into a clinch, striking shoulder against ribs, and with head resting under Sandel's left arm, Sandel almost invariably swung his right behind his own back and into the projecting face. It was a clever stroke, much admired by the audience, but it was not dangerous, and was, therefore, just that much wasted strength. But Sandel was tireless and unaware of limitations, and King grinned and doggedly endured.

Sandel developed a fierce right to the body, which made it appear that King was taking an enormous amount of punishment, and it was only the old ringsters who appreciated the deft touch of King's left glove to the other's biceps just before the impact of the blow. It was true, the blow landed each time; but each time it was robbed of its power by that touch on the biceps. In the ninth round, three times inside a minute, King's right hooked its twisted arch to the jaw; and three times Sandel's body, heavy as it was, was levelled to the mat. Each time he took the nine seconds allowed him and rose to his feet, shaken and jarred, but still strong. He had lost much of his speed, and he wasted less effort. He was fighting grimly; but he continued to draw upon his chief asset, which was youth. King's chief asset was experience. As his vitality had dimmed and his vigour abated, he had replaced them with cunning, with wisdom born of the long fights and with a careful shepherding of strength. Not alone had he learned never to make a superfluous movement, but he had learned how to seduce an opponent into throwing his strength away. Again and again, by feint of foot and hand and body, he continued to inveigle Sandel into leaping back, ducking, or countering. King rested, but he never permitted Sandel to rest. It was the strategy of age.

Early in the tenth round King began stopping the other's rushes with straight lefts to the face, and Sandel, grown wary, responded by drawing the left, then by ducking it and delivering his right in a swinging hook to the side of the head. It was too high up to be vitally effective; but when it first landed King knew the old, familiar descent of the black veil of unconsciousness across his mind. For the instant, or for the slightest fraction of an instant, rather, he ceased. In the one moment he saw his opponent ducking out of his field of vision and the background of white, watching faces; in the next moment he again saw his opponent and the background of faces. It was as if he had slept for a time and just opened his eyes again, and yet the interval of unconsciousness was so microscopically short that there had been no time for him to fall. The audience saw him totter and his knees give, and then saw him recover and tuck his chin deeper into the shelter of his left shoulder.

Several times Sandel repeated the blow, keeping King partially dazed, and then the latter worked out his defence, which was also a counter. Feinting with his left, he took a half step backward, at the same time uppercutting with the whole strength of his right. So accurately was it timed that it landed squarely on Sandel's face in the full, downward sweep of the duck, and Sandel lifted in the air and curled backwards, striking the mat on his head and shoulders. Twice King achieved this, then turned loose and hammered his opponent to the ropes. He gave Sandel no chance to rest or to set himself, but smashed blow in upon blow till the house rose to its feet and the air was filled with an unbroken roar of applause. But Sandel's strength and endurance were superb, and he continued to stay on his feet. A knock-out seemed certain, and a captain of police, appalled at the dreadful punishment, arose by the ringside to stop the fight. The gong struck for the end of the round and Sandel staggered to his corner, protesting to the captain that he was sound and strong. To prove it, he threw two back airsprings, and the police captain gave in.

Tom King, leaning back in his corner and breathing hard, was disappointed. If the fight had been stopped, the referee, perforce, would have rendered him the decision and the purse would have been his. Unlike Sandel, he was not fighting for glory or career, but for thirty quid. And now Sandel would recuperate in the minute of rest.

Youth will be served—this saying flashed into King's mind, and he remembered the first time he had heard it, the night when he had put away Stowsher Bill. The toff who had bought him a drink after the fight and patted him on the shoulder had used those words. Youth will be served! The toff was right. And on that night in the long ago he had been youth. Tonight youth sat in the opposite corner. As for himself, he had been fighting for half an hour now, and he was an old man. Had he fought like Sandel, he would not have lasted fifteen minutes. But the point was that he did not recuperate. Those upstanding arteries and that sorely tried heart would not enable him to gather strength in the intervals between the rounds. And he had not had sufficient strength in him to begin with. His legs were heavy under him and beginning to cramp. He should not have walked those two miles to the fight. And there was the steak which he had got up longing for that morning. A great and terrible hatred rose up in him for the butchers who had refused him credit. It was hard for an old man to go into a fight without enough to eat. And a piece of steak was such a little thing, a few pennies at best; yet it meant thirty quid to him.

With the gong that opened the eleventh round Sandel rushed, making a show of freshness which he did not really possess. King knew it for what it was—a bluff as old as the game itself. He clinched to save himself, then, going free, allowed Sandel to get set. This was what King desired. He feinted with his left, drew the answering duck and swinging upward hook, then made the half step backward, delivered the uppercut full to the face and crumpled Sandel over to the mat. After that he never let him rest, receiving punishment himself, but inflicting far more, smashing Sandel to the ropes, hooking and driving all manner of blows into him, tearing away from his clinches or punching him out of attempted clinches, and ever when Sandel would have fallen, catching him with one uplifting hand and with the other immediately smashing him into the ropes where he could not fall.

The house by this time had gone mad, and it was his house, nearly every voice yelling: 'Go it, Tom!' 'Get 'im! Get 'im!' 'You've got 'im, Tom! You've got 'im!' It was to be a whirlwind finish, and that was what a ringside audience paid to see.

And Tom King, who for half an hour had conserved his

strength, now expended it prodigally in the one great effort he knew he had in him. It was his one chance—now or not at all. His strength was waning fast, and his hope was that before the last of it ebbed out of him he would have beaten his opponent down for the count. And as he continued to strike and force, coolly estimating the weight of his blows and the quality of the damage wrought, he realized how hard a man Sandel was to knock out. Stamina and endurance were his to an extreme degree, and they were the virgin stamina and endurance of youth. Sandel was certainly a coming man. He had it in him. Only out of such rugged fibre were successful fighters fashioned.

Sandel was reeling and staggering, but Tom King's legs were cramping and his knuckles going back on him. Yet he steeled himself to strike the fierce blows, every one of which brought anguish to his tortured hands. Though now he was receiving practically no punishment, he was weakening as rapidly as the other. His blows went home, but there was no longer the weight behind them, and each blow was the result of a severe effort of will. His legs were like lead, and they dragged visibly under him; while Sandel's backers, cheered by this symptom, began calling encouragement to their man.

King was spurred to a burst of effort. He delivered two blows in succession—a left, a trifle too high, to the solar plexus, and a right cross to the jaw. They were not heavy blows, yet so weak and dazed was Sandel that he went down and lay quivering. The referee stood over him, shouting the count of the fatal seconds in his ear. If before the tenth second was called he did not rise, the fight was lost. The house stood in hushed silence. King rested on trembling legs. A mortal dizziness was upon him, and before his eyes the sea of faces sagged and swayed, while to his ears, as from a remote distance, came the count of the referee. Yet he looked upon the fight as his. It was impossible that a man so punished could rise.

Only youth could rise, and Sandel rose. At the fourth second he rolled over on his face and groped blindly for the ropes. By the seventh second he had dragged himself to his knee, where he rested, his head rolling groggily on his shoulders.

As the referee cried 'Nine!' Sandel stood upright, in proper stalling position, his left arm wrapped about his face, his right wrapped about his stomach. Thus were his vital points guarded, while he lurched towards King in the hope of effecting a clinch and gaining more time.

At the instant Sandel arose, King was at him, but the two blows he delivered were muffled on the stalled arms. The next moment Sandel was in the clinch and holding on desperately while the referee strove to drag the two men apart. King helped to force himself free. He knew the rapidity with which youth recovered, and he knew that Sandel was his if he could prevent that recovery. One stiff punch would do it. Sandel was his, indubitably his. He had outgeneralled him, outfought him, outpointed him. Sandel reeled out of the clinch, balanced on the hairline between defeat or survival. One good blow would topple him over and down and out. And Tom King, in a flash of bitterness, remembered the piece of steak and wished that he had it then behind that necessary punch he must deliver. He nerved himself for the blow, but it was not heavy enough nor swift enough. Sandel swayed but did not fall, staggering back to the ropes and holding on. King staggered after him, and, with a pang like that of dissolution, delivered another blow. But his body had deserted him. All that was left of him was a fighting intelligence that was dimmed and clouded from exhaustion. The blow that was aimed for the jaw struck no higher than the shoulder. He had willed the blow higher, but the tired muscles had not been able to obey. And, from the impact of the blow, Tom King himself reeled back and nearly fell. Once again he strove. This time his punch missed altogether, and from absolute weakness he fell against Sandel and clinched, holding on to him to save himself from sinking to the floor.

King did not attempt to free himself. He had shot his bolt. He was gone. And youth had been served. Even in the clinch he could feel Sandel growing stronger against him. When the referee thrust them apart, there, before his eyes, he saw youth recuperate. From instant to instant Sandel grew stronger. His punches, weak and futile at first, became stiff and accurate. Tom King's bleared eyes saw the gloved fist driving at his jaw, and he willed to guard it by interposing his arm. He saw the danger, willed the act; but the arm was too heavy. It seemed burdened with a hundredweight of lead. It would not lift itself, and he strove to lift it with his soul. Then the gloved fist landed home. He experienced a sharp snap that was like an electric spark, and simultaneously the veil of blackness enveloped him.

When he opened his eyes again he was in his corner, and he heard the yelling of the audience like the roar of the surf at Bondi Beach. A wet sponge was being pressed against the base of his brain, and Sid Sullivan was blowing cold water in a refreshing spray over his face and chest. His gloves had already been removed, and Sandel, bending over him, was shaking his hand. He bore no ill will towards the man who had put him out, and he returned the grip with a heartiness that made his battered knuckles protest. Then Sandel stepped to the centre of the ring and the audience hushed its pandemonium to hear him accept young Pronto's challenge and offer to increase the side bet to one hundred pounds. King looked on apathetically while his seconds mopped the streaming water from him, dried his face, and prepared him to leave the ring. He felt hungry. It was not the ordinary, gnawing kind, but a great faintness, a palpitation at the pit of the stomach that communicated itself to all his body. He remembered back into the fight to the moment when he had Sandel swaying and tottering on the hairline balance of defeat. Ah, that piece of steak would have done it! He had lacked just that for the decisive blow, and he had lost. It was all because of the piece of steak.

His seconds were half supporting him as they helped him through the ropes. He tore free from them, ducked through the ropes unaided, and leaped heavily to the floor, following on their heels as they forced a passage for him down the crowded centre aisle. Leaving the dressing-room for the street, in the entrance to the hall, some young fellow spoke to him.

'W'y didn't yuh go in an' get 'im when you 'ad 'im?' the young fellow asked.

'Aw, go to hell!' said Tom King, and passed down the steps to the sidewalk.

The doors of the public house at the corner were swinging wide, and he saw the lights and the smiling barmaids, heard the many voices discussing the fight and the prosperous chink of money on the bar. Somebody called to him to have a drink. He hesitated perceptibly, then refused and went on his way.

He had not a copper in his pocket, and the two-mile walk home seemed very long. He was certainly getting old. Crossing the Domain he sat down suddenly on a bench, unnerved by the thought of the missus sitting up for him, waiting to learn the outcome of the fight. That was harder than any knock-out, and it seemed almost impossible to face.

He felt weak and sore, and the pain of his smashed knuckles warned him that, even if he could find a job at navvy work, it would be a week before he could grip a pick handle or a shovel. The hunger palpitation at the pit of the stomach was sickening. His wretchedness overwhelmed him, and into his eyes came an unwonted moisture. He covered his face with his hands, and, as he cried, he remembered Stowsher Bill and how he had served him that night in the long ago. Poor old Stowsher Bill! He could understand now why Bill had cried in the dressing-room.